# A plan for freedom

"Day after t'morrow afore sunrise, we gonna leave this place."

"Day after t'morrow?" Mama asked.

"Yes'm . . . and cain't none of y'all whisper a word, send no one a farewell look with your eyes. Y'all go about your work like ain't nuthin' changed. Save any extra bits of bread, hoecakes and the like; nuts, roots, whatever you can get a hold of without bringin' attention to yourself."

Abraham climbed out of bed and sat cross-legged on the floor near the fire. "We headin' north, clear outta 'Merica to Canada, like you was sayin'?"

"Naw . . . south to the big swamp. Then clear into Florida if need be."

"And if'n we get caught?" Mama asked.

"We got two choices, Dessa," Pa replied. "Stay here and watch whilst Abraham and my Sally girl get carted off in the back of a wagon, or run away to freedom, all the while prayin' that the Lord keep and guide us."

Mama stared into the crackling fire, the flames dancing in her eyes. She was silent for a spell. Then she whispered, "Run away to freedom."

# My Name Is
 Sally Little Song

Brenda Woods

PUFFIN BOOKS

PUFFIN BOOKS

Published by the Penguin Group

Penguin Young Readers Group, 345 Hudson Street, New York, New York 10014, U.S.A.

Penguin Group (Canada), 90 Eglinton Avenue East, Suite 700, Toronto, Ontario, Canada M4P 2Y3
(a division of Pearson Penguin Canada Inc.)

Penguin Books Ltd, 80 Strand, London WC2R 0RL, England

Penguin Ireland, 25 St Stephen's Green, Dublin 2, Ireland (a division of Penguin Books Ltd)

Penguin Group (Australia), 250 Camberwell Road, Camberwell, Victoria 3124, Australia
(a division of Pearson Australia Group Pty Ltd)

Penguin Books India Pvt Ltd, 11 Community Centre, Panchsheel Park, New Delhi - 110 017, India

Penguin Group (NZ), 67 Apollo Drive, Rosedale, North Shore 0745, Auckland, New Zealand
(a division of Pearson New Zealand Ltd.)

Penguin Books (South Africa) (Pty) Ltd, 24 Sturdee Avenue,
Rosebank, Johannesburg 2196, South Africa

Registered Offices: Penguin Books Ltd, 80 Strand, London WC2R 0RL, England

First published in the United States of America by G. P. Putnam's Sons,
a division of Penguin Young Readers Group, 2006
Published by Puffin Books, a division of Penguin Young Readers Group, 2007

5  7  9  10  8  6  4

THE LIBRARY OF CONGRESS HAS CATALOGED THE G. P. PUTNAM'S SONS EDITION AS FOLLOWS:

Woods, Brenda (Brenda A.)

My name is Sally Little Song / by Brenda Woods.

p.  cm.

Summary: When their owner plans to sell one of them in 1802, twelve-year-old Sally and her
family run away from their Georgia plantation to look for both freedom from slavery and a home
in Florida with the Seminole Indians.

ISBN: 978-0-399-24312-7 (hc)

[1. Slavery—Fiction. 2. African Americans—Fiction. 3. Seminole Indians—Fiction. 4. Indians
of North America—Florida—Fiction. 5. Florida—History—19th century—Fiction.
6. Georgia—History—1775–1865—Fiction.] I. Title.

PZ7.W86335Myn 2006

[Fic]—dc22  2005032651

Puffin Books ISBN 978-0-14-240943-5

Printed in the United States of America

To my granddaughter,
Alexandra Rose

My Name Is
Sally Little Song

## On a Plantation Way North
## of Waycross, Georgia, 1802

I was born in the summertime on a hot August night when Mama said the moon shone like the sun, big and bright, nearly round. We could never be sure of the day, but my mama and pa remember the month and can be certain of the year because every girl child born on this plantation in 1790 had to be named Sally. Our mamas and pappies didn't have any say. There's Sally Jane, Sally Lee, and me, Sally May. The Master's wife named us all and we all carry the Master's last name, Harrison.

I was four years old when I first worked the fields, toting water from before sunup to after sundown.

Eleven planting seasons have passed since I was born in this land Pa calls 'Merica.

My name is Sally May Harrison and I am a slave.

# PART I

 ONE

Mornin' come
But no sun
And quiet is everywhere
Then I hear raindrops
Fallin' hard on the roof
And I feel my big teeth
Part my lips as I smile
No cotton pickin'
No cornfields today
Me and brother Abraham
Might e'en get to play

The sound of rain on the roof opened my eyes. A bucketful of wet wind whirled through the cabin's wall hole and I studied the day, then softly sang, "Mornin' come, but no sun, and quiet is everywhere . . ."

I yawned big, wanting to stretch, but I couldn't budge without waking everyone. We were like four field mice twined together on our narrow straw bed. Mama was still asleep next to me, Pa cuddled beside her, close like two hands when you pray. My only brother, Abraham, who is a year older than me, was flat on his back beside Pa, snoring loud and hard. His huge mouth was wide-open, chest growing so big with every breath, it looked like it was about to burst.

The cabin walls are black with soot and it only takes ten of my footsteps to cross from one side to the other. But we have a porch where we can sit outside and feel like our world is as wide as the sky with all of its stars. Out back we have a garden where we grow cowpeas alongside red yams, okra, greens, and watermelons, which Pa refers to as August hams.

The fire in the fireplace had burned out, inviting the cold to fill the cabin. But tiny pieces of hot wood that look like orange lightning bugs lingered, resting atop the gray ashes.

Mama groaned and pulled the blanket up around her neck. "Is the fire out, Sally May?" she asked.

"Sur'nuf," I replied.

"It rainin'?"

"Yes, ma'am . . . and plenty hard."

Mama squirmed out of Pa's arms, stared into my eyes, and smiled. "No cotton t'day."

I gave her a giant grin. "Indeed."

She tied on her head rag and poked Pa with her elbow. "Titus," she whispered.

Pa opened one eye and glanced around the cabin for signs of daybreak. "It mornin', Dessa?" he asked.

"Indeed, and rainin'," Mama replied.

I giggled and repeated, "Plenty hard."

The laughter in Pa's belly had barely rolled its way to his mouth when the rain began to pour through the holes in the roof.

"Abraham!" Pa yelled as he leaped up and pulled on his britches.

Abraham woke with a start and slid onto the floor.

"Grab rags, youngin, straw too. And hurry b'fore the floor turns to mud," Pa said as he pushed through the door and stepped outside.

I crawled out of bed and peeped through the half-open door. The sky held the darkest of clouds, promising an all-day rain.

I smiled at Abraham before he went out. "We got a day off and it ain't e'en Sunday."

"What you got to look so happy 'bout? Corn and cotton fields still gonna be there t'morrow and ev'ry day after that. B'sides, I betcha the Missy'll call you up to the house to help tend her youngins or clean her pantry," he fussed, trailing behind Pa outside into the storm.

I gazed toward the big house and hoped he was wrong. The last time it had rained, the Missy'd had more help than she needed up at the house and Mama and I'd filled our day with quilting and chatter.

"Sally May?" Mama called as she piled kindling and wood in the fireplace. "Don't appear idle or the Master might likely sell you."

"Master ain't likely to sell no one and I know it," I replied. "Never has and never will. Master say you born on Harrison land, you sur'nuf gonna die on Harrison land." Young Master Harrison uttered those words nearly every Sunday morning before he rode off to church: "I am not like my daddy, God rest his soul. . . . After all, I am a Christian man and the Lord above owns my soul," he would add as he cracked his whip once, then again, and often a third time before his lazy brown-and-white speckled horse would begin its slow gallop, pulling the buggy that brought the Master, who had eyes that were blue like the sky, and his yellow-haired Missy to the brick church with the wooden cross that pointed straight up to heaven.

"Hush now," Mama said, "b'fore the devil hears you and makes it not so. And here, set the pail out to catch water. Save you from havin' to tote it from the well."

I set the pail down outside and watched as the raindrops began to fill it, plinkity plink, plinkity plink.

Mama joined me and looked up. "Likely it'll rain all day, clear to nightfall."

We stood in the doorway side by side, the fire behind us beginning to blaze again, rainwater and wind brushing our faces, a woman and her girl child. I was almost as tall as she.

Mama's skin is the same deep brown color as mine, though she would say there are no two colored folks with skin that matches, tone for tone. One has a pinch more red, another a thimbleful of yellow, that one over there a hint of blue with his black. Her face is beauty mixed with sweet, her nose broad and bold, her eyes nearly black, her lips curled with pleasantness. Her hips are wide with plenty of flesh, her fingers long, her hands as callused as many men's, her back beginning to bend.

Mama pressed a pig ear in my hand. "Run and be

quicker than lightnin'. Give Hannabelle the ear and tell her I need a cuppa meal. Tell her the ear's already been cured. Hannabelle . . . she got a weak spot for pig ears."

Folks who enjoy talking and spreading tales, including my pa, claim Hannabelle Harrison is the oldest slave in America. They say she was born in Savannah and that the Old Master paid twenty dollars for her when she was about my age. She's as scrawny as a newborn bird, with a twisted back and wrinkled skin that's thin and as yellow as a not-quite-ripe ear of corn. Her hair is long, straighter than the Missy's, and everyone whispers that she's more than half white. She hobbles around slowly because one leg is shorter than the other. Mama says that some of Hannabelle's mind is missing, gone to that place where minds go when you lose them.

The way Pa tells the tale, Hannabelle was a comely young gal, sometimes too sassy, and oftentimes too sweet. She worked up at the house, tending the Old Master and his sickly missus, eating what was left of their vidlins, sleeping in a real bed. She listened carefully to their secrets through any open door, gathered them up, and carried them down to the slave quarters with the dirty wash. And then one day, no one can say why, it occurred to Hannabelle to run off, back to Savannah, to search for her kin.

Of course, Old Master Harrison searched everywhere

 11

for the lovely Hannabelle, trailing her day and night, his hounds weaving their way through the woods, pursuing, their noses hunting for her scent until they found it. Then the Old Master dragged her back, gave her the whip until blood streamed, and broke one of her legs with his hammer. Pa said Hannabelle had screamed and wailed so loudly, she likely split every ear from Alabama to the Carolinas.

"Spoze you won't run off again, will you, Hannabelle?!" the Old Master yelled, his wild eyes glaring, waving the blood-soaked whip in one hand, the hammer in the other.

"Nossir," Hannabelle had whimpered.

I could only be grateful that the Old Master and his missus were long dead before I drew my first breaths, but stories of his evil nature still made me shiver and tremble.

Since then, Hannabelle has labored in the fields. "Waitin' on the Lord to carry me to freedom. Carry me to freedom today." She repeats the same words over and over as we toil day after day, plowing, planting, picking, glinting in the sun as it shifts its place in the sky.

I stepped outside and turned, gazing yonder and near at the tiny cabins, twelve in all. Smoke rose from every chimney, forcing its way upward through the raindrops into the clouds, making it hard to tell where one began and the other ended. As I scurried along, the mud sank beneath my bare feet, my footprints melting away almost as fast as I made them.

"What you want, gal, out in this here rain?" Hannabelle said as she cracked open her door. "Ain't you got good sense?"

"Yes, ma'am, you know I do, but my mama need a cuppa cornmeal for pone bread. She say to give you this here pig ear. Already cured."

Hannabelle snatched the pig ear from my hand and I stepped inside her cabin. It was just like ours except she had a real chair. She measured out a cup of meal from her bag, put it in a small rag, tied it up, and placed it in my palm. "Now git!"

"Yes'm," I replied. As I hurried back to our cabin, a ray of sunlight sliced through the clouds. I whispered a quiet prayer to the Lord. "Please keep the rain comin' . . . least till after the sun goes down."

"Get out them wet clothes," Mama said as she mixed the meal with water. "And stand b'hind the curtain, Sally May. You 'bout grown."

I slipped the only other dress I own over my head, pulled on a pair of Abraham's hand-me-down britches, and sat down in front of the fire with my knees tucked under my chin. There was one yam roasting in the blue and yellow

 13

flames and as it filled the cabin with its sweet smell, my mouth watered.

"For your pa," Mama said, knowing what I was thinking. Mama hummed for a while and then took to singing a tune. "Got a little yam that sure is sweet. Wish I had another for my Sally to eat."

Just as she took a piece of pone bread out of the frying pan and slipped it on my plate, Pa and Abraham burst in, shaking the water off their soaked clothes like two mangy dogs.

"Never see'd so much rain. Fields'll likely be soggy t'morrow. If'n the Missy ain't sent for y'all yet, ain't likely she will. . . . Y'all might even get two days' relief," Pa said as Mama placed two pieces of pone bread on Abraham's plate, and two on Pa's along with the yam.

"Abraham," Pa spoke as he ate.

"Yessir," Abraham mumbled with his mouth full.

"Master got horses in need of shoes. Time I learned you ironwork same as my pa learned me. Get you out them fields. Fill your belly in a hurry, boy, and ain't no point in puttin' on dry clothes . . . all this rain."

Pa had been a blacksmith since he was twelve or thirteen, and his arms were as strong as the iron he worked. The Master called him skillful and oftentimes loaned him out to other plantations and farms. Pa always returned full of tales of the sights and sounds he'd picked up on his way. Only a few of Master Harrison's slaves had ever seen a real town and Pa was one of them. He often found himself in the town of Waycross, and once, he'd been as far as Carolina.

Abraham and Pa stuffed the last pieces of pone bread into their mouths and rushed outside again.

"Shut the door, Sally May, b'fore the fire blows out," Mama said.

I replied, "Yes, ma'am," but before I could get it closed, a she-goat, full of milk, squeezed in, searching for a dry warm place. I held her still while Mama milked her, and when she finished, Mama poured some of the warm, sweet milk into my tin cup. I drank it fast and begged for more.

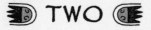 TWO

Like a grasshopper jumpin'
Between green blades of grass
A day can go too fast
Like bees from a hive
That's been rattled by a rock
A day can go too fast
Like a butterfly from your hand
To keep from bein' caught
A day can go too fast
Like a dark and rainy day
When cotton I won't pick
A day can go too fast

By the time night had come, the clouds were gone. A shining sliver of the moon and more than a hundred stars lit the sky.

"I could cipher clear to a hun'derd," I boasted to Abraham as he sat beside me on the porch step after supper. The wooden planks were soaked with water and I could feel my britches getting wet. But after spending all day inside darning and quilting, I didn't mind.

"You cain't not," Abraham replied. "Only white folks and the colored foreman could cipher clear to a hun'derd."

"I teached m'self," I said. "By countin' stars."

"How many there be t'night?" he asked, looking up.

"I dunno . . . too many to count . . . but more than a hun'derd. See?" I picked up a twig and pointed down into the wet dirt. I had made a hundred tiny marks, twenty sets of five, just like I'd seen the foreman do.

"Can you learn me?" Abraham asked.

"I dunno . . . so far I only teached m'self . . . but I could try." I handed him the twig. "Now look up and make a mark for ev'ry star. Make four marks, then when you get to number five, cross through the other four. That's how you know when you got five. Five and five makes ten. Ten and ten makes twenty."

Abraham stared up into the sky, looked down at the dirt, and made a mark. "How you know which one you ciphered? All of 'em looks the same 'cept some is big and others ain't."

"Keep both eyes on the sky when you make your marks," I said. "Make believe it's a giant pie that you dun cut a slice out of, then only count them that's in that slice. You cain't never count 'em all."

"One . . . two . . . three," Abraham paused. "Cipherin' ain't hard."

I watched a shooting star disappear into the sky and replied, "Never said it was."

"Hush up, Sally," Abraham said softly, his eyes still fixed on the sky. "Next thing I know, you gonna learn your letters."

"If'n I did, you 'spoze I could teach m'self to read'n'write?"

"More'n likely. You's quick-witted enough. Then you could write down them songs you and Mama's always singin'."

"One came to me this mornin' . . . wanna hear?"

"Sur'nuf," he replied.

I sang him my tune. "Like a grasshopper jumpin' between green blades of grass, a day can go too fast. Like bees from a hive that's been rattled by a rock, a day can go too fast. Like a—"

"Y'all come on inside now," Pa interrupted, standing in the door, gazing into the cloudless sky. "Sun gonna be up t'morrow."

"Yessir," we replied, and hurried inside.

We crawled into bed and sleep had just closed my eyes when someone knocked lightly on the door. Pa climbed out to see who it was. I could see a handsome face in the moonlight. It was Joshua.

Joshua worked up at the Master's house, serving and smiling, and almost always wore white gloves. The Missy made everyone who worked at the house wear white gloves, saying that was the only way she could tell whose hands were dirty and whose hands were clean. A girl named Lucinda who worked with Joshua had that as her main job, to keep the house slaves' gloves washed and white like new.

There were two things I fancied about Joshua. One was that even when I stood right next to him, I could hardly smell him, not like Pa, Abraham, and the other men who worked long and hard, sweat making streams down their backs, arms, and faces. The other thing was that whenever the four knuckles of Joshua's white-gloved hand rapped on our door, it generally meant he was about to slip Pa something sweet for us to eat.

"Much obliged, Joshua," Pa said as he took a small package from his hand.

"You welcome," he replied. "Master frettin' that the rain gonna ruin his harvest."

"Let him fret," Pa said.

Joshua laughed. "You right, Titus."

Soon Joshua's and Pa's voices became whispers and I couldn't hear what they were saying. That was usually how it was when Joshua came to call with a sweet treat or fresh secrets from the big house.

Abraham liked to tease me and told anyone who would listen that I was sweet on Joshua. But I didn't pay him any mind because Joshua was as old as Pa.

I had just conjured up a vision of myself with a husband who was young but sweet-smelling and good-looking like Joshua, and was feeling as happy as a bird with a plump worm in its beak, when I heard Joshua say, "G'night."

Pa shut the door, crawled back into bed, and opened the package. It held one big slice of ginger cake, which we shared before we curled up and went back to sleep.

The next morning, as Pa had foretold, the fields were too soggy to be worked. But just when I began to look forward to a morning to run wild and free, Mama told me that the Missy had chores for me to do up at the big house.

I knocked lightly on the big house back door and the always ornery Lucinda opened it. She was wearing a pair of the Missy's hand-me-down shoes and her usual smirk. " 'Bout time," was all she said as I stepped inside.

Lucinda was a year older than me. She had grown as stout as a full-grown pig from drinking whole glasses of milk fat and sneaking butter to spread on the bread that she stole from the Master's pantry. She was also snooty, the way the house slaves can be—except for Joshua, that is.

Lucinda kept her narrow nose pointed up in the air, looking like a hound trying to catch a scent. Oftentimes it occurred to me to remind her that she was still a slave, even if her hands and clothes were clean, but I never did.

"Missy says you's to dust," Lucinda said as she handed me a pair of clean white gloves and a dust rag.

"Dust what?" I asked as I put on the gloves.

Lucinda raised her voice. "Anything that needs dustin'!"

Joshua peeked out of the pantry and said, "Shhh . . . quiet now," then added, "Mornin', Sally May."

"Mornin'," I whispered.

"You best start upstairs . . . the Missy and her youngins is havin' their mornin' meal," Joshua said.

"Yessir," I said. I trudged up the stairs, making up a tune just like Mama does. Mama has little songs for almost every chore. She says it helps her keep her mind. "My bare feet on the wooden steps, to the top I go. Gotta dust what just got dusted only one day ago."

I slid my white-gloved hand along the banister until I reached the top of the steps and wandered into the Missy's bedroom. The bed was already made, pillows plumped, floor freshly waxed, lace curtains pulled back, and windows opened wide, allowing fresh air to fill the room. The toilet pot and the Master's spittoon were empty. I dusted everything, even though there was no dust to speak of, then went into the oldest girl's room.

She was called Miss Beatrice, and she had pink freckled skin, and brown hair that curled when the fog fell low. She was as tall as me, and laughed a lot. As I dusted her dresser, I was overcome with a weakness to open the drawers, and run my fingers over what I knew they held: her pretty belongings, fresh-pressed clothes, sweaters, socks with lace trim. But I was afraid someone would catch me, give me ten lashes with a switch or worse, the whip. So, the drawers remained closed.

I was just about to leave Miss Beatrice's room when I saw it. A book. I halted, then peeked into the hallway, listening for the sounds of people afoot. I didn't hear anyone, so I picked it up. I was looking at the letters, wondering what they said, when I heard someone behind me.

"What you doin', barefoot Sally?" It was Lucinda.

I closed the book and put it down. "Dustin' like I was told."

"That so? Seems to me you was lookin' at Miss Beatrice's book."

"Dustin' under it is all. What you want up here anyway? Ain't you got more gloves to wash?"

"Missy sent me. To keep an eye on you. Good thing she did."

"I's done in here," I told her. I stepped into the hall, but her eyes were still on the book. I stared at her, my eyes wide, as she picked up the book, tore out a page, crumpled it in her hand, and dropped it on the floor.

"What you do that for?" I asked.

Lucinda only laughed. And as she hurried down the steps, I knew the tattler's tale would quickly find the Missy's ears.

I was trying to smooth out the crumpled page when I heard the Missy call my name from the bottom of the stairs. "Sally May?"

"Yes'm?"

"Yes'm what?"

"Yes'm, Missy Harrison?"

"Come down here," the Missy said, her mouth twisted to one side by anger, Lucinda standing beside her, holding an iron, smirking.

"Yes'm, Missy Harrison," I repeated as I went down the steps. I had my hand behind my back, the page from the book in it.

I stood in front of her, so close that I could feel the warmth of her breath when she spoke, smell the tea she'd just drunk.

She spit another question at me. "Do you know your letters?"

"No, ma'am. You know I don't."

"Lucinda here told me you ripped a page out of one of Miss Beatrice's books. Is that so?"

"No, ma'am. It weren't me. It was—"

She didn't let me finish. "Hold out your hands," the Missy said harshly.

I did as I was told, the page from the book clenched tightly in my fist.

"Open your hand, gal!" she commanded.

The Missy took the now-damp page from my hand. "If you don't know your letters, why would you do this?" she asked.

"But I—"

"Shush!" Missy Harrison said.

I hung my head, knowing it was useless to try to convince her that it was Lucinda who had done it and not me.

"You know what happens when you do something like this?"

"Yes'm, Missy Harrison," I said. "Punishment."

"Hold out your hands again, faceup," she said.

"Yes, ma'am."

The Missy took the iron from Lucinda and held it over my hands. I felt the heat, and my body shook like a duck just out of water. I closed my eyes.

Just as she was about to burn my palms, Joshua spoke softly from behind her. "She'll be no good to no one, house or field, with hands all burnt and swole up, Missy Harrison."

Missy stared at me for quite a spell. Then she sighed. "I suppose you're right," she said, handing the iron to Lucinda. "But get me a thick switch, Joshua, and make sure it's still green . . . Sally May here has a lesson to learn."

Joshua bowed his head and complied. "Yes'm."

"Lucinda?" the Missy said.

"Yes'm, Missy Harrison?" she replied, grinning with delight.

"Finish up that ironing," she said as she handed her back the iron.

Lucinda skulked into the kitchen. I was glad she wasn't there to gloat as the switch passed from Joshua's hand to the Missy's. Joshua gazed into my eyes before he turned to join Lucinda. I hoped he had seen my gratefulness.

The Missy marched me outside. The grass was damp and soft under my feet. The switch hit my legs the first time, stinging. I flinched, gazing down as she circled me, hitting me from every side. I wanted to run away.

"Hold still, gal!" she warned me as she hit me again and again.

Tears welled up in my eyes and then ran down my cheeks. I could hear the switch cutting through the air, making a whizzing sound, then snapping as it met my flesh. The Missy didn't stop until my legs were bloody. It felt like forever.

Before she went inside, she pointed to a basket of just-washed sheets and said, "These need hanging."

I was trembling. "Yes'm, Missy Harrison," I replied, lifting a sheet from the basket and throwing it over the line.

I wished Lucinda dead, buried, and gone, but not to heaven.


That night, as Mama cleaned my wounds with warm water, I told Mama, Pa, and Abraham what had happened. Abraham shook his head and Mama said I should never touch anything that wasn't mine.

But few other words were spoken until Pa whispered, "Night, Sally girl."

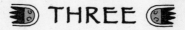 THREE

From up on his horse
The colored foreman says
Back to work y'all
We dun lost us two days
Straw hat on his head
New whip at his side
Gotta work fast
It's harvesttime

The sun felt like it was sitting on my back, trying to burn a hole clear through me. My legs were heavy from yesterday's beating and I dragged along, pulling my sack behind me. My lips were dry, my throat too. I searched the fields, hoping to see a little one coming toward me with a pail of cool well water. Better yet, I prayed, someone will offer me a slice of an August ham with its sweet pink juice and black seeds.

From one plantation to the next, this new crop called cotton seems to be taking over. The cotton itself is white, soft, and all fluff, but it's the prickly parts that surround the cotton meat that tear up your fingers. I hate it because it pains me, making my fingertips bleed so much that I almost miss picking, shucking, and grinding corn.

The colored foreman, his skin as black as the hair on my head, rode by slowly on his horse. "Y'all drink plenty water now," he advised. "Ain't no good to no one sick or dead."

Hannabelle was working behind me. I heard her whisper, "Waitin' on the Lord to carry me to freedom. Carry me to freedom today."

I stopped picking and wiped at the sweat streaming down the back of my neck. Pa's youngest sister, Delilah, was two steps ahead of me. "Why Hannabelle always says that . . . 'carry me to freedom'?" I asked.

Delilah stood up straight and rubbed the small of her back. "Askin' the Lord to let her die and take her up to heaven," she replied.

"Why come?"

"You ain't no heathen, is you, Sally May?" Delilah asked.

"No, ma'am, you know I ain't."

"Then you knows that the Lord is in heaven above, where He sits on His throne . . . and when we gets there, He gonna greet us and welcome us into the place called Paradise, where the streets is paved with jewels and gold and we gonna have everything: a house bigger than the Master's, plenty pretty clothes like the Missy and her little gals, all the sweets we could eat. We'll be smilin' and laughin', fulla joy, fiddle music in the air, folks dancin' and carryin' on . . ."

Delilah was grinning big and wide.

I gazed up at the clear blue sky.

Heaven sounded wonderful.

Suddenly, from across the fields I heard the colored foreman's voice and the hooves of his horse as he galloped toward us. "Dee-li-lah!"

Delilah started working fast, but the foreman already

had his whip out and I cringed as it snapped against Delilah's wet back.

I didn't look up when he spoke. "Dee-li-lah?"

"Yessir?" Delilah replied.

"Keep waggin' your tongue and I might take a mind to cut it out. What you tryin' to teach this youngin?" he asked.

"Nuthin'," Delilah replied.

He cracked his whip a second time. "Nuthin' who?"

"Nuthin, sir," Delilah said, arching her back in pain.

"Back to work . . . all y'all," he muttered.

I glared at him as he trotted away on his horse, wishing he would get the whip and feel its sting. I studied the pain on Delilah's face, ran my hands across my red, welted legs, and began to know why Hannabelle wanted to be as far away as heaven.

"He worse than the white foreman. I catches a gleam in his eye every time he snaps that whip," I heard Old Moses say as he slowly dragged a half-full sack of cotton behind him. Old Moses' fingers were twisted, his bushy hair white, his back covered with scars from the whip, his rotten teeth almost all gone.

"Take some, Sally May. It's fresh from the well and cold," a small boy named Little Pete said, dipping the ladle into the water pail and pushing it into my hand. He was missing his two front teeth. I watched him smile as the water cooled my burned purple lips. I dipped it in again and swallowed quickly. By the third time, I started to feel alive again.

"Much obliged," I said as I handed him back the ladle.

Delilah dipped both hands in his pail, splashed water on her face, and sighed. Her belly was huge with child and I knew that sometime soon there would be a knock on our door and a voice would whisper, "Dessa, come quick." Then Mama would rush out like a whirlwind, coming back a good spell later, bringing tales of the newest girl or boy child who had been named by the Missy and added to the Master's growing list. So far this year, only two girl children had been born, and both had been named Naomi. The first was called Naomi Louise, the second Naomi Marie. If Delilah had a girl, she would become Naomi number three. If she had a boy, no one could say what his name might be.

I'd been working all day but hadn't had anything to eat since morning except some roasted nuts Old Moses had given me. The sun was going down, sinking behind the trees into the earth.

Abraham was with Pa again, learning ironwork, and Mama was on the other side of the plantation. One of the old-timers who did nothing but grind corn in a shed had died last evening, so Mama had been given her job. It had only been one day, but I already missed them, Mama alongside me, spreading her sweetness through the fields, Abraham's heavy feet plodding behind me.

I glanced up at a flock of cranes flying south. Then I strained my ears, listening for frog music because by the time they begin croaking, it's almost time to head back to the quarter.

Suddenly Delilah yelled loudly, "Lord Jesus, help me!" and fell to the ground, moaning, arms around her big belly.

The foreman circled her on his horse. He commanded Old Moses and some others to put Delilah in the wagon on top of the burlap sacks full of fresh-picked cotton. "Get her back to the quarter, quick!" he told the driver, then turned to me. "Sally May, go get Dessa . . . tell your mama that Delilah's time is come . . . and make haste, gal."

"Yessir," I replied, and took off faster than a cottontail rabbit, holding my dress up so I wouldn't trip, the dusky air cooling my face.

I burst through the shed door where she was grinding corn. "Mama! Mama! Come quick!"

"What's the matter, child?"

"It's Delilah, her time is come and the foreman, he say to come quick."

The sun finished setting and the moon took its place in the sky as Mama and I hurried toward the quarter. "Fetch me two pails of water from the well, Sally May," Mama said as she entered Delilah's cabin.

Late that night, Mama tiptoed over our threshold, humming a soft sweet tune. "Delilah got herself a boy child. The Missy gived him the name Samson. His head's mighty big . . . almost lost both of 'em." Mama slipped out of her dress and climbed into bed alongside me.

"Ain't that sumthin', Samson and Delilah?" Pa mumbled, his mind half asleep, tongue half awake.

"Missy say she and Master leavin' early t'morrow, headed to Savannah. Say the Master's brother got troubles."

"That so?" Pa asked.

"Sur'nuf," Mama replied.

"I'll ask Joshua tomorrow," Pa grunted as he drifted toward sleep. "He'll likely know."

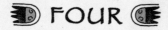 FOUR

The news spread in whispers
Late the next day
Master and the Missy gone
Up Savannah way
Not sure how long
They gonna be away
Brethren got worries
Is what they say

Delilah turned sickly in the three days since the baby came, and Mama had to be by her side. So I took Mama's job grinding corn into meal. The shed was cool like a spring morning and though I was pleased to be out of the sun, there was no one to talk to. So I made up another song.

"Grindin' corn, grindin' corn, grindin' corn ain't so bad. But pickin' cotton, pickin' cotton, pickin' cotton makes me sad." I sang it over and over as I ground the corn into meal and put it into sacks.

I was just working and singing, singing and working, the corn grinder humming, when out of the corner of my eye I saw something small and quick burst through the shed door. At first I thought it was a bobcat until I saw her. It was January July.

January July was nearly nine, scrawny like me, and everyone in the quarter, young and old, complained she was the laziest gal they ever knew. She was named January July by her mama and pa because she was born one January when the Master and the Missy were away. Then they added July because it just sounded right. So the white foreman had recorded it in the book, January July Harrison, and no one can tell you why, but the Missy never changed it.

"You 'bout scared the ghost outta me!" I yelled.

"You scareda everything, Sally May," she teased.

"Is not," I said.

"Is so."

"What you run in here for?" I asked. "Hidin' from the foreman agin?"

January July grinned. "Sur'nuf."

"Might as well help me then," I told her.

"Don't know how," she replied.

"I could learn you . . . see. You put the dried corn in here and turn this handle. And when the meal comes out here, you put it in one of these sacks."

January July grabbed a handful of yellow kernels and spilled them into the grinder. "Like this?"

"Yessiree," I said, and started singing again. "Grindin' corn, grindin' corn, grindin' corn ain't so bad—"

"What you singin'?" January July asked.

"A song I made up."

"Why come?"

"To help me keep my mind."

"Where could it go?"

"Somewheres."

"Who telled you that?"

"My mama."

But when I started singing the corn song again and January July joined in, I suddenly wished I didn't have ears to hear. Her voice sounded like two crows cawing.

"January July, you cain't hardly sing."

"I knows," she chuckled.

The sound of rolling wheels and horses' hooves made us stop working and peek through the tiny window. Alongside the corn shed was a narrow road that divided Harrison land from the Sullivan plantation across the way. Two white men, one with bright red hair, both carrying rifles, rode beside a wagon that was being driven by a third white man. In the back of the wagon sat a huge colored man, chain around his dark thick neck, his body bloody, face bloodier. His head was held down like he was barely alive. One of the white men jabbed him with his rifle and the huge colored man sat up straight.

"Stay alive, nigger," the white man said. "We got a big bounty to collect."

I whispered to January July, "A runaway."

She replied softly, "Sur'nuf."

"They's sure to hang him," I told her.

"Why come?"

" 'Cause he run off," I replied, and returned to grinding corn.

"Then he gonna be dead?" she asked, still peeking through the window.

"Dead as could be."

January July shook her head. "I ain't never runnin' off."

I agreed. "Neither me."

January July loaded more kernels into the grinder, and as we ground the corn, we sang, "Grindin' corn, grindin' corn, grindin' corn ain't so bad . . ."

Later that night, as the fire flickered, I told the story of the runaway.

"Likely they'll hang him," Pa said.

"You ever ponder runnin' off, Pa?" Abraham asked.

Mama put her finger to her mouth. "Shhh."

"Cain't nobody hear us, Dessa," Pa said.

"Well, did you?" Abraham asked again.

"Yessiree, a heap of times. Ever since I was a youngin I been lis'nin to tales of colored who made it North, some all the way outta 'Merica clear to Canada, where there ain't no such thing as slavery. I even hear'd tales 'bout folks who tried to go back to Africa."

"Africa . . . where your pa come from?" I asked.

"Sur'nuf, Sally girl, clear across the ocean." Pa got a dreamy look in his eyes. "I see'd it once from the shores of Carolina."

"Africa?" Abraham asked.

"Naw, son. The ocean. Piece of water that carries your eyes as far away as the moon."

I leaned my head on Pa's shoulder. "That where Africa is . . . far away as the moon?"

"Seems to me it just might be."

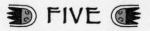 FIVE

Master been sour
Like vinegar they say
Since him and the Missy
Come back thissa way

Little more than a fortnight; that's all it's been since Delilah's boy child, Samson, was born. But Delilah's already back to work. The cotton fields are only half picked, but the corn is nearly harvested, row after row of yellowing stalks swaying with the wind.

Joshua has been down to the quarter most evenings since the Master got back from Savannah. Last night he and Pa sat on the porch, whispering until sunrise. Pa keeps a worrisome look, and Mama tells us to let him be because he's pondering hard and deep. Pondering what, she can't say.

That night, when Joshua knocked softly, Mama and Abraham were deep asleep, but I was wide-awake. When Pa went outside, I crept to the door, peeked through an eye-sized hole, and listened.

"Only five, I heard the Master say: January July, Abraham, Sally May, L'il Pete, and that big gal from up at the house, Lucinda. I gotta say I'm glad she's goin', though it'll likely be hard on her mama and pappy."

"You sure you heard right?" Pa asked.

"I ain't deaf, Titus. Plus I even see'd it wrote down."

"Didn't know you could read."

"Just a mite," Joshua replied.

"Go south, you say?" Pa asked.

"Past Waycross."

"Into the big swamp?"

"Indian land. Called Seminoles . . . and from what I hear, they's likely to help you. What I been told is that colored is free to live amongst 'em long as they work the land and give a portion of their crop to the chief. In return, they gives you protection from the white man."

"So is the coloreds slave or free?"

"From the tales I been told, the Seminoles claim cain't no man own another." Joshua hesitated. "And I also been assured that white men and most slave hunters ain't too fond of the swamp. But don't be fooled, Titus. Some Indians is crafty, working with bounty hunters and the like. So you best beware."

Pa kept quiet for a while before he asked another question. "All 'cause of fever?"

"Sur'nuf, nearly wiped out his brother's whole quarter, young and old, stout and lean. Gotta help him, he say . . . 'boutta lose his crops . . . made a solemn promise to send him five of his slaves in less than a fortnight."

"But why my boy and Sally May?" Pa sounded like he had tears in his eyes. "Think it's 'cause of Lucinda and that book?"

Joshua glanced away from Pa, up at the half-moon that was hanging in the sky. "Cain't say."

"The four of us'll be gone afore sunrise day after t'morrow. You got the canteen and vidlins?"

"Sur'nuf . . . and I'll bring another canteen and more provisions for y'all t'morrow," Joshua said as he handed Pa two sacks. "Make sure y'all steer clear of Waycross and try and keep close to the water's edge. Makes it harder for them heartless hounds to catch your scent."

"I'll remember," Pa replied.

"And . . ." Joshua hesitated again. "Be watchful of gators . . . I hears they got 'em monstrous big. Able to swallow you whole in one bite. And snakes—they got cottonmouths and rattlers that can kill you quick as a whistle."

"I'm beholdin' to you, Joshua."

"May the good Lord keep you, Titus," Joshua replied. "You been better'n a brother to me. I'll surely miss you."

"Then come with us, Joshua," Pa said.

"Naw, Titus. Runnin' . . . it ain't for me. B'sides, I ain't never been a brave man. You was always the brave one. Maybe it's where you belongs, with the Indians. They's a brave people, and proud too, from what I'm told."

Before Joshua turned to walk away, he gave Pa's shoulder a long squeeze. By the time Pa came inside, I had scrambled back to bed, pretending to be asleep.

Pa whispered our names. "Dessa, Abraham, Sally May?"

Mama lifted her head from the pillow. "It ain't sunup yet, Titus."

"I know, but I got something to tell y'all. Day after t'morrow afore sunrise, we gonna leave this place."

"Has you lost your mind, man?" Mama asked.

"Naw, Dessa, I still got my mind. But Master 'boutta send Sally May, Abraham, and three other youngins to his brother in Savannah."

"For how long?" Mama asked.

"For always," Pa replied.

Abraham laughed. "You must be funnin' with us, Pa."

"It's truth . . . Joshua even see'd it wrote down."

I sat up in bed, remembering the runaway January July and I had seen from the shed, beaten, bloody, and nearly dead. Worry filled my mind. Would that happen to us?

"Day after t'morrow?" Mama asked.

"Yes'm . . . and cain't none of y'all whisper a word, send no one a farewell look with your eyes. Y'all go about your work like ain't nuthin' changed. Save any extra bits of bread, hoecakes and the like; nuts, roots, whatever you can get a hold of without bringin' attention to yourself."

Abraham climbed out of bed and sat cross-legged on

the floor near the fire. "We headin' north, clear outta 'Merica to Canada, like you was sayin'?"

"Naw . . . south to the big swamp. Then clear into Florida if need be."

"And if'n we get caught?" Mama asked.

"We got two choices, Dessa," Pa replied. "Stay here and watch whilst Abraham and my Sally girl get carted off in the back of a wagon, or run away to freedom, all the while prayin' that the Lord keep and guide us."

Mama stared into the crackling fire, the flames dancing in her eyes. She was silent for a spell. Then she whispered, "Run away to freedom."

## SIX

Gotta look down
Into the dirt all day
Or my brown eyes
Is sure to give us away

he next morning, I was in the fields just as the sun peeked into the sky. Birds flew overhead, calling to each other with their songs, and two cottontail rabbits crossed my path. I told myself, don't talk, keep your head down, and pick fast.

Delilah was the first to notice. "What's wrong, gal, your eyes ain't met mine all mornin'. You still broodin' over that whuppin'?"

"Yes'm," I said.

"Pickin' cotton mighty fast," Old Moses said, smiling and nearly toothless.

"Yessir," I replied, staring into the dusty dirt beneath my feet. "You got some peanuts?" I asked him.

"Sur'nuf, little gal. Always got a handful or two for you," Old Moses replied, and placed them in my outstretched palm. He raised his eyebrows as I slipped them into the pocket of my dress, not eating them right away, the way I generally did.

"Savin' 'em for later," I told him.

"Suit y'self," he said.

That was when I saw January July doing something she hardly ever did—picking cotton. I dragged my sack full of cotton to the wagon, hoisted it into the back, and grabbed an empty sack. Seeing that the foreman was nowhere around, I made my way to the place where January July was picking. I wondered what she'd do if she knew that someday soon she would be taken away, never to see her mama and pa or three brothers and two sisters again.

When one of the little ones touched her back, trying to draw her away from the fields and into a game of tag, she arched her back in pain. I could tell she had gotten it. The whip.

I inched up behind her. "You aw'right?" I asked.

January July's eyes searched the fields for the foreman before she spoke. "Naw . . . got twenty licks."

Blood oozed through the back of her dress. "I's sorry," I said.

She punched a fistful of cotton into her sack. "Why come? You ain't the one gived me the beatin' . . . Master did."

I didn't believe my ears. Master hardly ever gave the whip to anyone, usually leaving that dirty work to one of the foremen. And I'd never seen him beat a child. "Master?" I asked.

"Yes'm. Then he told me I cain't be no lazy gal no more, runnin' off, hidin' till suppertime."

A trail of tears rolled down January July's cheek. I wanted to warn her, to tell her to tiptoe to our cabin tonight and I would beseech Pa to take her with us. But instead I kept the secret as I had been told.

"I got some nuts . . . Old Moses gived me," I told her, reaching into my pocket. "You could have 'em if'n you want."

"I ain't hungry, Sally May," was all she said as she pulled her bag full of cotton toward the wagon.

I made my way back to my row, taking my place between Delilah and Hannabelle, gazing into the blue sky, wondering how far away the sun was and how far we were going to have to run. I glanced at January July and sadness filled me. I heard a horse trotting and got back to work.

But it wasn't the foreman. It was the Master, wearing clean, pressed clothes. I flinched when he came to a stop in front of me and called me by name. "Sally May?"

"Yessir," I replied, staring at the hooves of his horse, whose iron shoes were thick and new, fashioned by my pa.

From his saddle, the Master cast a dark shadow. "You're a good little worker and I thank you," he said, and tipped his hat.

I was tempted to look up, but didn't dare. "You's mighty welcome, sir."

As he rode away, I knew that was his way of saying good-bye. But thinking back to the whipping and the hot iron the Missy had held over my hands, I felt not a bit of sorrow. I was glad tonight would be my last on Harrison land. I only wondered about the big swamp where we were headed and the Indians Joshua had said would help us.

It was nightfall before the foreman let us go back to the quarter. January July walked up beside me. I took her by the hand and led her to her cabin.

"Good-bye," I told her.

"Why come?" she asked.

"Why come what?"

"Why come you said good-bye when you gonna see me t'morrow? You oughta just say g'night."

"Sorry, g'night," I said as she went inside.

"Night, Sally May!" Delilah called as she glided past me, holding her baby boy, Samson, anxious to nurse him, then rock him to sleep.

"G'night," I replied.

Hannabelle hobbled by. "Waitin' on the Lord to carry me to freedom," she whispered.

"My pockets is fulla plenty," Abraham said as he butted into the cabin. "Looka here. I got nuts, roots, pieces of pig fat, plenty dandelions, and every yam big and small from the garden."

"Anyone see'd you?" Mama asked.

"Naw . . . 'cause I was quick as quick can be."

Pa pushed through the door, carrying two large sacks. "Compliments of Joshua."

I peeked outside, into the night, hoping to catch a glimpse of him so I could wave so long.

"We 'boutta leave?" Abraham asked.

"Naw, folks is still about. We gonna eat, then rest a spell."

My insides felt like bugs were crawling through them, and my hand shook when I picked up my cup to fill it with water.

Abraham laughed. "Sally May got a case of the nerves."

Pa patted my head. "She got a right to have the nerves . . . we all does. This land right here is all she ever knowed, you and your mama too. And we goin' to a place ain't none of us ever see'd b'fore. So you let your sister alone, boy . . . she's the only one you got."

"Amen," Mama added.

Pa got on his knees. "We gonna pray."

We knelt in front of the fire and Pa prayed. "Lord above . . . You know why we gotta leave this place and we beseech You to guide our feets, to keep us safe from hurt and harm. Send Your mighty angels to be our guides and please bless those we's leavin' b'hind. Amen."

" 'Specially January July," I added.

"Indeed," Mama whispered.

We ate without speaking, then lay down on the straw bed. But I kept my eyes open, watching the flames dance on the soot-covered walls. I was scared. Scared we might get caught. Scared of the woods at night. Scared.

After a while, Pa sat up and said softly, "Dessa, Abraham, Sally May . . . it's time. Y'all get up and make haste."

Mama whispered a question. " 'Tis the right thing to do, Titus?"

" 'Tis . . . and be quiet as deer," Pa said as we tiptoed away from the cabin.

# PART II

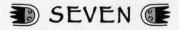 SEVEN

Runnin' fast
No lookin' back
Runnin' hard
Gotta keep on
Bleedin' feet
No never mind

We ran into the cornfields, past the cotton fields, each of us glancing over our shoulders at the faintest sound, flinching at the slightest movement, our footsteps guided only by the light of the moon. We each carried a sack and by the time we'd made it to the place where the fields turned into the woodlands, mine was already feeling heavy. I turned, taking one last look at the Harrison plantation, the place that had been my home.

"Joshua say we gotta follow that star," Pa said.

"Which one?" Abraham asked.

Pa pointed at the sky. "The biggest one . . . right there."

I looked up. It was as if it was the only star in the sky. "I sees it, Pa."

Pa picked up speed. "C'mon, we got a long ways to go."

We trotted like horses into the woods. Pa led, me right behind him, Mama trailing me, Abraham on her heels, running fast, faster, faster, out of breath, gasping for air, darting between low-lying branches of trees, stepping in gopher holes, losing our footing, getting it back again. Rocks and branches cut my feet, but I was too scared to feel any pain.

We ran for what felt like forever, chomping on pieces of pone bread and pigskins when we got hungry. By the time morning came, we were deep into the woods.

We sank into a clump of tall grass. Pa said, "Y'all sleep now, while the sun is shinin'. When darkness comes, we'll run again."

"You sure, Titus?" Mama asked.

"Harder for 'em to see us runnin' at night."

"You right," she replied.

"Now, if you's finished frettin', Dessa, go to sleep. Me and Abraham gonna take turns keepin' one eye open."

"We's just like possums, sleepin' in the day, scoutin' around in the dark," Abraham said, and leaned his back against a tree that was oozing sap.

"Owls and bats too . . . they only flies at night," I added as I curled up beside Mama.

"Shush now," Pa advised.

Before I closed my eyes, I saw Pa pull something out of one of the sacks Joshua had given him. It gleamed as the sunlight bounced off of it. A knife with a long blade.

It was almost evening when I woke up. Abraham was snoring, Mama was deep asleep, and Pa was nowhere to be seen.

I squirmed out of Mama's arms and circled the tree Abraham was sleeping under, trying to be as quiet as a kitten. But Mama still woke up. She brushed the leaves and dirt from her clothes. "Where's your pa?"

"Don't know. I just waked up and he was gone."

Out of nowhere, we heard the sound of footsteps atop dry leaves. Mama placed her hand over my mouth and pulled me behind the tree. And as the footsteps got closer, I felt Mama tremble, but I couldn't keep myself from peeking. It was Pa.

Mama saw him too. "What you tryin' to do, Titus, scare me and this child outta our wits?!"

"Naw, Dessa . . . don't be so fainthearted." He placed his arm around her shoulders. "I located us a creek and some gooseberries." He opened his hand and showed us. "They's mighty sour, like gooseberries always is. I was hopin' to find some blackberries, but I was plum outta luck."

I took one of the tiny berries from his hand, swallowed it, and frowned.

"The canteen's fulla fresh water. Take a swallow, Sally May," Pa said.

It was some of the sweetest water I'd ever tasted.

Abraham finally woke up and Pa chided him. "Wasn't you told to keep one eye open, youngin?"

"I tried, Pa . . . but either I had to keep both of 'em open or both of 'em closed."

"So you decided havin' both of 'em closed was best?"

"Yessir, I did."

None of us could keep from laughing loud. For a twinkling we were happy and free. I wondered if this was what it was like in Delilah's heaven.

Then, as quick as a jackrabbit being chased by a fox, it was over. Pa stared at us. "Anything happens to me . . . y'all gotta press on. Swear to me, Dessa."

"I swear b'fore you and the Lord, Titus," Mama replied.

"And Abraham . . . you's a man now. Understand?"

Abraham stretched. "Yessir, I do."

"Thissa way." Pa motioned. We followed him to the creek, watching, listening. "We'll wait here a spell till the sky gets good and dusky."

When darkness fell, I searched the sky for the star and pointed. "There it be . . . Joshua's star."

"Joshua's star? That the name you gived it, Sally May?" Pa asked.

"Yessir."

" 'Cause you's sweet on him, huh?" Abraham snickered.

"Naw . . . 'cause he's the one who told Pa."

Pa agreed. "Then Joshua's star it is."

"When you spoze we'll get to the swamp, Titus?" Mama asked.

"From what Joshua told me, it'll likely be three nights if we's quick, four if we's slow."

"How he knows so much?" Abraham asked.

"From workin' up at the house all these years, travelin' with the Master and Missy to Waycross, Savannah, Macon, once clear to Virginia, keepin' his big ears open."

Mama grinned. "He sure do have some big ears."

Pa laughed. "Who you tellin'?"

"Why we headed south 'stead of north, clear outta 'Merica to Canada, like you talked 'bout?" Abraham asked.

I knew the answer but I held my tongue.

"Like I told y'all afore, it's too far and it's tricky. More'n likely the four of us wouldn't make it."

"But why the swamp?" Abraham asked.

"Indians."

Mama glanced at Pa. "Indians?"

"Joshua say they's likely to help us. Say they let you live with 'em and round about 'em. He say they e'en let some colored join their tribes."

"Colored Indians?" Abraham asked. "No sucha thing."

"Called Black Indians."

Mama turned, looked back toward the plantation, and asked, "Who else the Master planned to send off?"

"January July, big Lucinda from up at the house, and L'il Pete," I blurted.

Pa halted dead in his tracks. "How you knowed that, Sally May?"

I told the truth. "I sneaked outta bed and heard you and Joshua talkin'."

"So Joshua ain't the only one got big ears?" Mama asked.

"Spoze not," I answered.

We started trudging through the woods, over soft grass, around fallen branches and anthills, stepping on pieces of tree bark and moss, catching glimpses of bats and owls flying in the moonlight, of coons and possums scurrying. Then I heard them.

"Pa?" I said. "I hear hounds."

We halted and listened.

"You hearin' things, Sally May. Ain't no hounds," Abraham scoffed.

"Shhh," Mama said.

We kept quiet until one of the bloodhounds let loose a howl.

"They's far yonder, hurry now," Pa said, and started trotting. The wind was blowing and we galloped into it.

"We ain't goin' back," Mama said, panting. "I'd rathers be dead than live without my youngins."

"Ain't no one 'boutta be dead. We gonna make it. I knows we will," Pa said as we came to a riverbank. "More than one way to outsmart them mangy hounds. Y'all follow right b'hind me and keep both feet in the water along the bank of this here creek."

We dragged our feet through the shallow water, crisscrossing through the creek. I pictured the hounds catching me, biting my arms and ankles, pulling me to the ground. "Run faster!" I said.

And we galloped again, taking giant strides, until we no longer heard the sounds of the hounds and the sky had changed color to the blue that comes right before the sun.

Finally, we slowed to a walk. "Thissa long creek," Abraham said, scratching his arms and back. "And the bugs dun bit me up good."

Pa laughed. "Stop whinin', boy. You worse'n a little gal."

I poked Abraham in the back with the tip of a stick I'd been carrying. "Worse'n a little gal," I taunted.

Abraham grabbed the stick from my hand and waved it at me. "I'ma give you a lickin', scrawny gal."

"I ain't afeared of you, Abraham . . . you and your big feets," I said, prancing around him until he fell in the water. I laughed hard. "Big feets, big feets, big feets!"

"I ain't payin' you no mind, Sally May," he said.

"Stoppit!" Mama scolded. "Here we is runaways and y'all behavin' like it's Sunday b'fore last."

Pa pulled Abraham to his feet. "Y'all save your fussin' for after we's outta harm's way."

Abraham glared and warned me. "I'ma get you, Sally May. Just wait and see."

"I spoze we can stop callin' you Sally May . . . seein' as you's the only Sally out here." Mama gestured toward the thick woods and yonder. "Spoze we can just call you Sally from here on in. What you think, Titus? I never did care for the name of May, but the name Sally got a sweetness to it."

Pa agreed. "So Sally it is."

Mama started humming and that led to a song. "Got a child named Sally, sweet as could be, likes to sing little songs, just like me."

I smiled and held her hand.

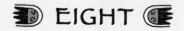 EIGHT

Sun big and bright
Wind through the trees
I closed my eyes
And dreamed

We slept beside a slow-moving creek where the water barely covered the speckled rocks. I dreamed I was a big plantation Missy, still colored but a Missy. I had a fine house, petticoats with white lace, dresses with red ribbons, pretty parasols, and a pantry full of food and sweet candies. All day long I sat on the veranda with my feet up, sipping lemonade, while white folks and Lucinda waited on me hand and foot.

I was truly enjoying my dream until the smell of cooking vidlins woke me. Pa was roasting a big fish. I rubbed my eyes. "How long I been sleep?"

"Quite a spell, Sally May."

"It's just Sally now," I reminded him.

Pa apologized. "I's gonna try hard to remember, but would you forgive me if I forgets sometimes?"

"Yessir, Pa," I replied.

His eyes had circles under them, dark like a coon, and I could tell he was tuckered out. I glanced over at Abraham. He was snoring. "I could keep one eye open for you while you rest," I told him.

"Just one eye?"

"Nossir, both."

"You sure, little gal?"

"As could be."

"Have a piece of fish with me and then I'll lay my head down . . . but if'n you hear them hounds, rouse me straightaway."

"I will, Pa."

While the three of them slept under a willow tree whose branches brushed the ground and swayed with every breeze, I listened for the sounds of dogs and horses ridden by slave hunters.

I softly whistled and watched as a big beaver waddled up to the water's edge to drink, but the sounds of birds overhead made me look up at the sky, which was bluer than blue. I thought about January July, how she couldn't carry a tune, and smiled. Then I remembered that any day now they were going to carry her away.

All of a sudden a rustling in the brush made me jump. But it was just a white-tailed deer headed to the creek. I studied it as it put one small hoof in front of the other, looking this way and that, the way deer tend to.

One more night until we reach the big swamp, Joshua had said, the big swamp where snakes and gators lived. That was the last thought I had before I leaned against the wide tree I was sitting under, closed my eyes, and fell asleep.

"Sally," Pa whispered as he grabbed my sleeve and

pulled me behind the trunk. "Get up in the tree," he said, pushing.

"Huh?" I said, shaking the sleep off.

Abraham reached out his hand and pulled me up to the branch where he was sitting. "Shhh," Ma said from up in the tree, pointing to three hounds on the other side of the creek.

The thickness of the leaves hid us from their view, but I caught glimpses of the dogs as they sniffed the air, turning around in circles, confounded.

I heard Mama praying softly as two white men riding horses approached the hounds and pointed at the trees near where we were hiding. One of them had bright red hair, and as they led their horses to the edge of the creek, I realized they were the same two men January July and I had seen from the corn shed. Slave hunters.

But just as they readied to cross the creek, two golden foxes darted out of the woods behind them. The foxes pranced along the creek bank, leading the bloodhounds away from us.

"Darn hounds! Ain't worth the slop you feed 'em!" the man with the red hair hollered. They glanced toward the tree where we were hiding one more time before they turned their horses, following the foxes and barking dogs.

 77

It was a long while before we dared to climb down from the tree. Mama and I held each other and cried. The color had left Abraham's face and sweat poured down his back and arms. We gathered around Pa, scared, tired, and trembling.

"Titus . . . oh, Titus," Mama whimpered.

"Y'all hurry. Gather up your things," Pa said, and we darted into the brush.

I followed on his heels. "I's sorry, Pa."

"For what, Sally?"

"For closin' my eyes and lettin' sleep catch me." I hesitated. "And for pickin' up that book, bringin' all this trouble."

"Cain't say it was the book, cain't say it wasn't," was all he said.

For the first time since we'd begun our journey, we didn't wait until nightfall to continue. We weaved through the woods, trying to be as quiet as could be. I tripped over knotted tree roots and fell hard. Pa pulled me to my feet. "You hurt?"

I was, but I said, "Naw, Pa," and kept running. My knees were scraped and burning, but the air cooled them.

Soon I felt like a bird, my feet flying over the earth, but the air got harder to catch. I stopped and doubled over, hands on my knees. My heart raced and my chest heaved, gulping for air. My throat was raw and dry. Mama stopped beside me.

"C'mon!" Pa called.

"She cain't, Titus. She cain't. She's still a child. You runnin' like you got hot coals 'neath your feets." Mama held me, taking each breath with me.

"She's right, Pa," Abraham panted. "Cain't no one run fast as you."

Pa gave up, let us rest, and after a spell Mama asked, "How we gonna know when we gets to the swamp?"

"Water . . . spoze there'll be plenty of it," Pa replied. "And gators," he added. "Got some so big, they's able to swallow you whole with one bite."

Mama frowned. "Who told you such a thing?"

"If'n it's a tale, Joshua told it," he responded, glancing up toward the sky. "Hope we's headed in the right direction. Joshua's star ain't out yet to guide us."

"Maybe we should wait till dusk, Titus," Mama advised.

Pa listened for the hounds, and hearing none, sighed and agreed. We slumbered awhile until darkness finally came and the moon fell into the sky, along with plenty of stars, including Joshua's.

We started trotting again, this time more slowly, until Mama halted. She got wide-eyed as she looked far yonder, past a clearing, and grabbed Pa's hand. "Titus, what's them lights?"

"Waycross . . . that be Waycross, Georgia. That means the swamp cain't be much further. And we gotta steer clear 'cause they got lawmen and slave hunters." Pa changed direction and motioned. "Hurry!"

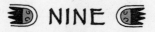 NINE

Grass wet
Beneath my feet
Owls say
Hoot
Night bugs fly
Snakes wriggle
Gators chomp
Swamp

We'd been heading east for many miles to get away from Waycross. Now Pa searched the sky for Joshua's star. We cautiously changed direction to follow it.

"This here grass be a mite soggy," Abraham said. "This the swamp?"

"Sur'nuf," Pa replied. "This the swamp. And y'all be watchful for snakes. They got plenty . . . some with rattlers, some not. Got one called a cottonmouth—can kill you quick."

"Why they call it a cottonmouth?" Abraham asked.

"Inside of its mouth looks like cotton," Pa replied.

"You think them Indians got cotton fields?" I asked.

"I dunno," Pa grumbled.

"If'n they do, you think we gonna havta pick it?"

"Dunno that neither, Sally."

"What kinda Indians we lookin' for?" Abraham asked.

"Called Seminoles," Pa answered.

"They gonna find us or we gonna find them?"

"Cain't say," Pa replied.

"They speak Indian or same as us?" I asked.

"Cain't say that neither," he said. "Thissa way." Pa motioned.

Mama tugged on Pa's shirtsleeve and uttered words I'd never heard her say before. "I's awful tired, Titus."

Mama sank to the ground. Pa pulled her to her feet. "You's strong, Dessa."

But Mama cried, "No, not no more! I's tired of being strong . . . been stronger than iron all my days."

Her crying turned to wailing. Pa wiped at her tears and wrapped his arm around her. "Cain't stop now," he said, leading her along. "You can make it."

I grabbed her other hand and reassured her. "We gonna be just fine, Mama."

Abraham was three steps behind us. "Just fine, Mama," he repeated.

I almost believed him until they flew toward us like a swarm of bees, screeching. Bats. We swatted at them, ducking one way, leaning another.

Right then, I missed the wooden porch, warm fire, and small straw bed of our cabin. But I didn't dare tell Pa. I just trailed behind him, hoping that wherever we were going to would be better than where we'd come from.

Mama stayed quiet as we stepped through the soaked grass. When we came to a small lake, she finally spoke. "Never see'd trees like these, growin' outta water. They sure is lovely."

"Cypress trees," Pa said.

The black water of the lake was a mirror, showing us a picture of everything that sat above it, including the moon. "It's real pretty, Pa, ain't it?" I said.

"Sur'nuf," he replied, and added, "but the day's 'bout to break through. Y'all hurry, no time to dawdle. When we find a dry spot, we'll stop and get our bearings."

"And some shut-eye?" Abraham asked as we trailed along.

"And some shut-eye," Pa replied.

"I sure hope we finds them Indians quick," I added.

"Me too," Pa replied.

When the sun came up, Pa led us to a big patch of dry green grass alongside a small lake. He smiled. "Just like a prairie."

Mama sat down under a tree. I snuggled up close to her, listened for the sounds of barking dogs, and hearing none, closed my eyes.

By the time I woke up, it was after midday and everyone else was still sleeping. I inched away from Mama, put my hand over my brow to shut out the glare of the sun, and looked yonder for Indians. I didn't see any, but I quivered when I saw a snake with skin that looked like a rainbow wriggling through the tea-colored water. I waited until it had gone by before I cupped my hands and drank. Swamp water.

As I drank, the sky began to darken, and I headed back under the tree, figuring rain was about to come. I kept watch while it rained gently. Just as quickly as the rain and clouds had come, they disappeared and the sun shone bright again.

Then, from out of nowhere, a bobcat showed up on the water's edge. While the cat lapped at the water, I scooted toward Pa.

"Pa," I whispered.

"Huh?"

I pointed. "A bobcat."

Pa sat up. "Shhh . . . they's shy as could be. Keep still. Soon as he gets his fill, he'll run off."

After the cat had crept away, Pa said, "Water must be safe to drink."

"It tastes real good," I informed him.

"How long you been awake, Sally?" he asked as he drank from the swamp.

"A spell."

"See'd any gators?"

"Nossir," I said. "Don't think so. All I see'd was a snake with skin that looked like a rainbow and now that cat. What they look like, anyhow?"

"Gators? Like a lizard but black and huge . . . bigger'n some men, with a broad snout and plenty sharp teeth."

I must have looked scared, because Pa patted my shoulder and told me not to fret about the gators.

"Thissa strange place, Pa."

" 'Tis," he replied. "Got flowers and trees that could grow in nuthin' but water."

I waved my hands back and forth in the water, making ripples that traveled farther and farther away. "And them ain't ducks," I said, pointing at a flock of birds in the lake.

"Naw, little gal. They's coots and they's good eatin'."

"I's plenty hungry, Pa. Wish I had a yam. E'en some pork bellies."

"Me too . . . if we's lucky, we'll catch us a wild turkey," Pa said hopefully.

My mouth watered. "A turkey?"

"Sur'nuf. But for now, we gotta make do with what we can find nearby."

I picked at my fingernails. "Is we gonna die?" I asked.

"Nossiree," was all he said, and I wanted to believe him.

"Is they gonna catch us and carry us back to the plantation?"

"No indeed," he replied. Pa's body suddenly shook. Beads of sweat covered his forehead.

"Is you feelin' poorly, Pa?"

"Naw, Sally girl . . . just a chill," he replied as his body quivered again. At the same instant, Abraham woke up, yelling like a bolt of lightning had struck him. "What's the matter, boy?" Pa asked.

I taunted him. "Pro'bly got a heap of red ants in his pants."

"Naw, scrawny gal . . . I been dreamin'."

"Musta been an awful dream," Pa said.

"Yessir, plum awful. I was hanging from a tree."

"With a rope round your neck?" I asked.

"Sur'nuf."

"Have mercy," I replied.

"Y'all quit it now and help me find some eats," Pa said.

By the time Mama woke up, Pa had caught us a big fish with a spear he made and two coots by snaring them as they waddled in the prairie grass. Abraham and I had gathered up a mess of dandelions, a bunch of wild berries, and purple fruit from a tree we had never seen the likes of.

"Look what we found," Abraham said as he showed the purple fruit to Mama and Pa. "They kinda looks like plums, and I bet they's just as sweet," he said, preparing to take a bite.

But Pa snatched the fruit from his hand. "Might be fulla poison, boy . . . I swear you ain't got a licka sense!"

Abraham got a beaten-down look on his face and sat in the grass.

"Don't be hard like a hammer, Titus. The child be hungry," Mama chastised Pa as she stroked the top of Abraham's head.

"Don't none of y'all eat nuthin' you ain't ate b'fore," Pa warned.

I glanced over at the two birds that were roasting over the fire. "What 'bout them coots?" I asked. "I ain't never ate no coot."

"Well, I has, and they's safe to eat," Pa replied. Then his eyes took on an odd look and he fell to the ground.

"Titus!" Mama called, rushing to his side, trying to rouse him. "Titus!" she said again, but couldn't wake him. She frowned when she touched his forehead. "Fever."

We helped her drag him under a tree and for a time we watched the breath go in and out of him. "Is it a bad fever, Mama?" I asked.

"Got all kinds, some kill you, some cain't," she replied as she ripped off a piece of her dress. "Soak this with water, wring it out, and bring it back. Gotta keep his head cool, what my mama taught me."

Pa's body shook with chills. "Lord, please don't let my pa die," I prayed as I raced toward the water.

Abraham offered Mama his help. "What you need me to do?"

"Hand me the blanket. Nuthin' else to do but keep his

body warm, head cool." She glanced at the roasted coots. "Y'all eat now. All I can hope is that whatever dun took a hold of him don't git the rest of us." She paused. "Either of y'all feelin' outta sorts?"

Abraham placed the back of his hand on his head. "No, ma'am, not me," he replied as he pulled the tender cooked coots apart.

I touched my head. It was burning hot. Mama could tell by the look on my face that I had the fever too.

"You's on fire, Sally, ain't you?" she asked as I sat down beside her.

"Yes'm," I replied. "Could be the water. Me and Pa was the first to drink it."

"Cain't say," Mama replied as she tore off another piece of her dress and handed it to Abraham. When he brought the soaked cloth back, she laid me down, put my head in her lap, and placed the cool compress over my eyes and brow. "Rest now, sweet gal . . . rest now," she said softly as she rocked me back and forth.

# ⟫ TEN ⟪

His arm round her waist
Frogs croak
Her head on his shoulder
Crickets keep time
A full moon above
Night dancin'

By the time I woke up, it was almost evening of the next day and Pa was gone. "Is Pa dead?" I asked Mama.

Abraham answered, "Naw, scrawny gal, cain't nuthin' kill Pa. He's off scoutin', searchin' for Indians. You the one we thought was gonna die, talkin' in your sleep, singin' a song 'bout grindin' corn. If'n you hadn't been so sick with fever, I woulda laughed so loud, they woulda heard me clear back to the plantation."

Mama gave me sips of water from the canteen. "You hungry?" she asked.

"Yes'm," I replied. "Y'all eat all the coot?"

Abraham rubbed his stomach. "Yes indeed, and it sure was good."

"But we got plenty fish and the sweetest raspberries that ever touched my tongue." Mama smiled as she stroked my hair.

"And me and Pa caught some frogs . . . tastes like chicken," Abraham boasted.

"I don't havta eat no frog, do I, Mama?"

"No frog, but you gotta eat sumthin' b'fore you waste away," she replied.

"Yeah, 'cause you's scrawnier'n ever. E'en them frogs got more meat on their legs than you," Abraham teased.

I tried to get up so I could chase him, but my legs wouldn't hold me and I fell back to the ground. "Careful now," Pa said from behind me, and I turned around to see him smiling big. "Fever 'bout gone?"

"Sur'nuf, but she's more than a mite weak, too weak to walk," Mama answered.

Abraham interrupted, "You see'd any Indians?"

"Naw, but I see'd gators big and small. They's unsightly creatures. See'd a black bear too. I figure from here on in we's best to travel while the sun is up. We'll stay the night here, but t'morrow we gotta make up for lost time."

Two white birds with long, thin orange legs waded in the lake where dragonflies hovered and flowers bloomed.

Above us a black vulture circled.

That night, Mama and Pa danced under the light of the moon, to the music of the night. And for the second time since we'd left Harrison land, I smiled.

The next morning, I stood up carefully, hoping my legs would hold me.

"You gonna be weak for a spell," Mama said.

"You able to walk, Sally?" Pa asked. " 'Cause if you cain't, I could carry you."

"I could walk, but not run," I replied.

After we ate some berries and dandelion roots, Pa studied the rocks he had used last night to make an arrow to point us in the right direction. He looked yonder, then tossed the stones this way and that.

"Why come you did that?" Abraham asked.

"Trackers and slave hunters . . . don't wanna leave 'em no clues. And make sure the fire's out good."

While Abraham doused the fire, Pa pulled off a leafy branch from the cypress tree and dusted the brush where we'd camped. Mama questioned him. "Thought you told us white mens was afeared of the swamp?"

"It's what I was told, but we cain't be careless," he said as he led us away from the prairie, into the tall wet grass. I was on the lookout for black bears, big gators, poison-fanged snakes, and bobcats.

We passed mounds of moss-covered earth where plants and trees grew.

"Don't y'all think about tryin' to walk on it," Pa warned. "I tried and it trembled b'neath me. It ain't real land, just moss, peat, and plants sittin' atop the water."

When a hawk soared overhead, Pa proclaimed, "Looka that: We's free! Free as birds!"

"Feels good, don't it?" Mama added.

"Sure do, gal," Pa replied, laughing, his teeth white and gleaming in the sun.

I stared at the tips of my fingers. Gone were the cuts and pricks made from cotton plants. I glanced at my legs. Gone were the welts and scars from my whipping. I felt like a pig who'd been let out of the pen, a chicken who'd squeezed its way out of a coop. Out here in the swamplands everything roamed free, including me.

"Is we slaves or is we not?" I asked.

Pa replied, "We's free!"

## ELEVEN

Two vultures
Circling above
Like flies
Round a stirring spoon
Shoo I think

We hurriedly made our way through the high blue-green grass, around the thick trunks of cypress trees, over brooks, through rocky creeks, along riverbanks where the water ran fast. A sound drifted from far, far away in the distance and found my ears, a howl as long as a yawn. "You hear that, Pa?" I asked.

Pa listened carefully. "Naw, nuthin'."

"Howlin'," I whispered.

"Pro'bly a wolf, Sally," he replied. "But you keep them ears open good, just in case."

We waded through the murky swamp, stopping once to rest our sore, swollen feet and search for vidlins that we gobbled down, barely chewing, before we started on our way again. At first, the water of the swamp had only covered our feet, then our ankles, and just before sunset, it was up past me and Mama's knees. I was still weak, and after losing my footing the third time, Pa made me climb on his back. But no matter which way we took, we couldn't seem to find a dry spot.

"Looka yonder!" Pa said, pointing to a patch of prairie in the near distance.

We were rushing toward land when I saw the hump of

its spiny black back. From what Pa had told me, it had to be a gator, a gator as big as Abraham.

"Pa!" I screamed. "A gator!"

Pa swirled around and tumbled face-first into the swamp. I let go of Pa's neck and stood in the now waist-deep water.

Mama dropped her sack and darted through the water toward me, her arms flailing, drawing the attention of the creature.

Abraham yelled, "Sally!" and pulled me toward land.

Mama struggled, trying to reach us, but fell. "Dessa!" Pa called out, making huge strides toward her.

Mama pushed herself to her feet. Pa reached for her hands.

"Titus!" Mama screamed as the swamp water around her turned bloody. The gator had gotten to her first.

I opened my mouth to cry out, but no sound came. Abraham rushed through the water to help. Pa pulled out his knife and stabbed the gator, piercing the gator's thick bumpy skin with his knife again and again. Then he slit its throat and the gator gave up the fight.

As the gator's lifeless body floated in the shallow bank, Pa and Abraham dragged Mama to land. The sun was setting and cranes and coots flew overhead. I stared at the bloodred water and cried. "Mama," I whispered as I knelt beside her in the soft grass. "Mama," I repeated.

Mama moaned. There were two huge gashes in her leg and a small one on Pa's arm.

Pa tore off his shirt and tied it tightly around Mama's leg. "To stop the bleedin'," he told us.

"Y'all ain't gotta look so worried," Mama said. She sat up, saw the gaping wounds, and her face turned sour, her eyes heavy with gloom.

"You gonna be fine, Dessa. Lay back and rest your mind while I decides what we gonna do."

"We gonna keep on," Mama said, trying to stand up.

"Don't e'en try, Dessa," Pa warned her. "Gator bit clear through, broke the shinbone. You dun lost a heap of blood, gal."

Mama shivered. "I's cold as could be, Titus."

"Hurry, now, and build a fire," Pa told Abraham.

"Yessir," Abraham said as he ran off to gather wood.

"Maybe we dun wrong, leavin' the plantation . . . we ain't had much but trouble since we run off," Pa said.

Mama tried to console him. "Quiet now. I gonna be just fine. Take more than the bite of some ornery creature to put me in the ground." Mama turned her head to me. "How you feelin', Sally?"

"I's fine, Mama," I told her, but it was a lie. I was tired and weak as could be. I untied the shawl from around my shoulders and draped it over Mama's leg. "To keep the bugs and critters away," I said.

Pa glanced at the gator. "Joshua told me they make good eats," he said, pulling out his knife again.

The sacks filled with our last provisions had sunk or drifted off and the only things that remained were the canteens that had floated to the surface. Still, I pursed my lips. "I ain't gonna eat it."

Pa looked toward the gator again. "It's all we got, Sally girl," Pa said. "You strong enuf to help gather wood?"

"Yessir," I replied. By the time I got back with an armload of branches and twigs, Mama was sitting up, her back resting against a tree, and Pa was waiting with fresh gator meat. The fire Abraham had built came to life, flickering, and I eavesdropped from behind the tree.

"If'n I die, Titus—" Mama began.

"You ain't gonna die, sweet gal," Pa replied.

"But if'n I do . . . y'all got to go on. Find them Indians or let them find y'all. It would please me if'n my youngins was free or close to it. You hear me?"

"I hear you, but I ain't payin' you no mind, Dessa."

"And don't think you gotta be lonely. Take another wife. Bein' alone don't suit most menfolk."

"I ain't listenin' to your foolish talk," Pa replied.

"You ain't listenin', but I knowed you hear'd me, man," Mama said, caressing the back of his leg.

I stepped from behind the tree. "You thirsty?" I asked Mama, offering her the canteen.

"Sur'nuf." After she'd had her fill of water, she added, "I loves you, gal . . . always will."

I tried hard to smile. "I know, Mama . . . I loves you too."

Later that evening, we chewed on tough gator meat, surrounded by quiet, until weariness drifted us to sleep. When morning came, I awoke to find Pa kneeling over Mama.

My heart turned over twice as I rushed to his side. "She dead?"

"Naw, but I cain't wake her and her leg dun already gone black from lack of blood." Pa lifted my shawl from her leg. "Cain't say I know what to do. Your mama be the doctor."

I put my ear to Mama's chest. "Her heart's beatin', but slow."

"Sally?" Mama opened her eyes and whispered, "Gimme sip of water."

Pa lifted her head as I brought the canteen to her lips. "Where's my boy?" she asked.

"Abraham!" Pa yelled.

Abraham woke up and ran toward us. Mama reached

for his hand and he knelt beside her. "You's a good boy . . . always was . . . never no trouble to no one," she told him.

"Thank you, ma'am," he replied, and kissed her cheek.

"I'ma rest now," she said as she closed her eyes.

We hovered around her. Mama's breathing slowed. She panted before it slowed again. Then she stopped altogether.

Pa shook her body gently. "Dessa? Wake up."

But she didn't and I knew.

My mama was dead.

Pa rocked her back and forth in his arms. "She dead?" Abraham asked.

Pa shook his head yes.

Abraham bolted away and I started after him. "Let him go . . . it be his way," Pa said.

Pa held her close and closed his eyes tight, like he was trying to keep his tears inside, but they burst through, flooded his face, and he wailed loud, hard, deep.

"Don't cry, Pa," I told him. "Likely she's already in paradise with a big house and plenty pretty dresses."

"Sur'nuf," he replied. "Singin' one of her little songs."

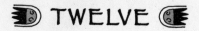 TWELVE

Mama
Sweet Dessa
In heaven
Gone

We buried Mama's body in the swamp. The red earth was wet and parted gently, allowing us to put her deep in the ground. We still covered her grave with stones to keep the vultures and critters away. Once we finished, we prayed, gathered under a tree, our bodies knotted together, and sobbed until sleep caught us.

At daybreak the wind carried birdsongs and the sounds of voices to my ears. At first, I reckoned it was Pa or Abraham talking in their sleep. Then I heard the voices again and sat up. There were two men, with skin the color of fresh pecans, standing near the water's edge over the body of the dead gator.

I shook Pa's shoulder. "Pa," I whispered. "Indians?"

Pa lifted his head. "Sur'nuf," he replied.

Abraham opened his eyes. "Mama?" he asked, speaking for the first time since yesterday.

"Naw, boy . . . your mama's gone," Pa reminded him.

The Indians now stood in front of us, one stout, the other tall.

Abraham jumped to his feet and screamed, "Have mercy!" Pa stood in front of Abraham and me, guarding us.

The Indians had green paint under their eyes and beads of many colors around their necks. Their straight black hair was long with head rags tied around it, but only in the front; their private parts covered with animal skins clear to their knees, their chests bare. They carried spears. I didn't dare move.

The tall one examined the gash in Pa's arm, and pointed toward the dead alligator. *"Alpata?"* he said.

"Yessir . . . gator," Pa replied.

The stout one went over to where Mama was buried. *"Ist-ey?"* he said, pointing at the wooden cross that Pa had fashioned.

I suppose Pa figured he wanted to know who was buried there. He patted over his heart and gestured toward Abraham and me. "My Dessa . . . their mama," he told him.

"Mama?" he asked, staring at us sadly.

Pa sighed. "Yessir, Mama."

*"Alpata?"* He seemed to be asking if the gator had killed her.

"Yessir, *alpata,*" Pa replied in their tongue, and pointed to the dead gator.

The two Indians exchanged words, and rushed to where the dead alligator lay. They pulled two long, narrow boats out of the brush toward the water. *"Aw-ita!"* the tall one said, and motioned as if to say, "Come."

Pa took my hand, but I glanced at Mama's grave and pulled him back. "I wanna stay here . . . with Mama!"

"Also me," Abraham echoed. "Why we gotta go with them Indians? They cain't e'en talk English."

*"Aw-ita!"* the stout one yelled.

"Your mama's with the Lord," Pa said, dragging me along.

I dug my heels into the ground, fighting him. "Naw, Pa . . . naw!"

Finally, Pa picked me up and put me in the tall Indian's boat. After he and Pa pushed it into the water, they climbed in with me.

Abraham and the stout Indian shoved the other boat along the bank and slipped into the river behind us. Pa held me tight and whispered in my ear, "Be still now, sweet gal, and stop frettin'. It's what your mama wanted."

The Indians pushed into the river bottom, using long poles, and the boats skimmed atop the water alongside each other, fast, faster. I stared back at the place where Mama was buried and screamed, "Mama!" The boats cut through the river, making their way deeper into the shady swamp, through places where trees grew so close together, the sun barely shone, and the leafy branches hung so low, it was hard to see in front of us.

Through my tears, I studied the tall one. He had pictures painted on his strong arms and shining rings in the flesh of his ears. His feet and legs were wrapped with animal hide. I wondered what kind of place they were taking us to. Swarms of dragonflies darted out of our way as the boats moved on, and I sank into the arms of my pa.

I was just about to close my eyes, hoping sleep would take me away, when a fish jumped out of the water and landed in my lap. I stood up and screamed, rocking the narrow boat so much, it nearly tipped over.

The tall Indian laughed, staring at me with eyes that were as black as coal. He motioned for me to sit back down.

"Pa," I said, "I's afeared," all the while watching the fish flip around in the boat this way and that.

"Ain't nuthin' gonna harm you, Sally girl," he replied.

The stout one called out, *"Ya facca!"* and gestured as if to say, "This way."

The tall Indian turned our boat, trailing closely behind him until in the distance we saw land and the light of day. We pulled up to the water's edge, and he motioned for us to get out. After the Indians hid the boats in the thicket, we followed them closely, stepping on their shadows, along a well-beaten trail, toward their village.

# PART III

 THIRTEEN

Under the sun
Ears of corn
Freshly picked
Bake
Women cook
While tag and such
The little ones
Play

We gathered stares from everyone, young and old, as we followed the two who had brought us here to a house that had no roof. A huge fire blazed and Indian women, wearing beads, capelike blouses, and colorful skirts, stood cooking. The women's hair was combed into flat rolls on the tops of their heads. Small children darted in and around, covering their mouths to hide their smiles.

Every footpath seemed to lead to where we stood. Yonder, I saw smaller houses, probably thirty in all. They sat on legs high off the ground and had roofs made from leaves. It looked so different from the plantation that I wondered if we were still in 'Merica or if somehow we had made our way to another land.

One of the women who appeared older than me but younger than my mama gestured for us to come sit near the fire. She placed leaves and pumpkin shells that held a heap of vitlins in front of us. She was brown, but many shades lighter than me, wearing plenty of beads that looked like a colorful collar around her neck.

"Much obliged," Pa said.

"Yes'm, thank you," Abraham whispered.

"Thank you, ma'am," I added, staring into her kind eyes, trying hard to return the smile she gave me. The pumpkin shells reminded me of Mama's cooking, but I was too hungry not to eat.

As the smiling woman fed the fire more wood, Abraham observed, "She kinda look like us . . . colored, don't she?"

Pa glanced up at her from his food. "Cain't say."

I nibbled on dried meat and yams, and sipped soup I could tell was made from ground corn.

"More?" the smiling woman asked as she approached Pa.

"You speaks English," Pa noted.

"Yessir," she said shyly.

Abraham stopped eating. "Who learned you?"

"My mama and my pa too—he was colored."

"Runaway?" Pa asked.

"Yessir, but he's dead six years now."

"You speak Indian too?" Abraham asked.

"Yes, my mama . . . she's a Seminole, still alive."

"Got a lot of colored here?" Pa inquired.

She held up five fingers. "Two were bought by our chief from the Spaniards. And some are part colored, part Seminole . . . some villages have more . . . some less . . . some none. Some colored have their own villages with their own chiefs, but they're farther to the south."

Pa stopped eating, leaned back as if his insides were full, and kept talking. "Is they free?"

"Most come and go as they please—help with the village fields, planting, harvesting crops, gathering roots, berries and such, hunting, fishing, trapping, making canoes. Some have fields of their own, and they're obliged to give a portion of their harvest to the *Mekko*. If there's war or white soldiers come, bringing us harm, the men are asked to fight . . . till death if need be."

Pa nodded. "I understand, and we's much obliged to your people for bringin' us here."

"If ever you are hungry, there is always a pot of *sofkee* on the fire, which burns day and night." She paused, then added, "You all should rest now. Later, after the sun has set"—she gestured toward Pa—"you will meet our *Mekko*."

"*Mekko?*" Pa asked.

"Our chief."

She led us to one of the houses with a leaf roof. It was midday and the sun beat down, but the inside of the house felt cool. The part-colored Indian gal grinned and said softly, "I am called Smiling Deer."

"Pleased to meet you, Smiling Deer," Pa said. "This be my son, Abraham, and this my girl child, Sally. I be called Titus, Titus Harrison."

"And your missus?" she asked.

There was a long silence. I finally spoke. "Dead . . . all 'cause a gator bit her."

"But Pa took his knife to the gator and slit its throat." Abraham gestured.

"I am sorry," Smiling Deer whispered. "Rest now," she added before turning to walk away.

I curled up on one of the straw beds, but before I closed my eyes, I turned to Pa. Tears were shining in the corners of both of his eyes. "Dessa," I heard him say.

It was dark when Smiling Deer woke me and offered me clean clothes. I followed her to a creek, where I washed my hair and body.

"Before you dress, rub this on your skin," she said, and put what looked like pig grease in my hand.

I sniffed it. "Look like pig grease, but it ain't got the same smell."

"Bear fat and honeysuckle. A little in your hair will keep it soft."

Dressed in a skirt and blouse that was almost just like Smiling Deer's, I followed her back into the center of the village to the house where the cooking and eating were done, where the fire blazed day and night. Abraham and Pa were dressed like Indians too, eating, drinking, their eyes wide.

Abraham glared at me as I sat beside him. "I feels naked without britches, like a sheep with no fleece." He shook his head and stared into the dirt. "B'sides . . . this ain't pleasin' to me."

"What ain't pleasin' to you?" Pa asked.

"That we's alive, got bellies fulla food, and Mama . . ." His voice trailed off and he sprang up and bolted away.

I was about to chase him, but Pa tugged on the hem of my skirt and said, "Let him be, Sally."

I sat back down and murmured one of my songs. "Like a grasshopper jumpin' between green blades of grass, a day can go too fast."

"That's it, gal, sing you a little song."

"It's what Mama taught me . . . keeps you from losin' your mind."

"Then sing all the songs you needs to, Sally May."

"Just Sally," I reminded him, and started singing again. "Like a butterfly from your hand to keep from bein' caught, a day can go too fast."

One of the old, wrinkled Indian women hobbled over and stood in front of me. *"Yaheyk-ick-is,"* she said.

Smiling Deer came over. "She says, 'You are singing.' "

Then the old woman turned to her. She must have asked her my name, because Smiling Deer told her, "Sally."

"Sally *Cotk-i Yaheyk-ita,*" the old woman said to me.

"She knows no English, only our Seminole tongue. But

she says she has a name for you already: Sally Little Song,"
Smiling Deer said.

"Tell her my name be Sally Harrison," I said.

Smiling Deer spoke to her, but the old woman kept repeating the words in Indian that meant "Little Song" as she toddled away.

My eyes darted around. I was wearing Indian clothes, eating Indian food, but I sure wasn't an Indian. I was colored through and through. I lowered my head and pictured folks I'd most likely never see again: Old Moses, slipping roasted peanuts into my hand; Hannabelle, snatching a pig ear; Joshua, handing Pa a piece of sweet ginger cake; January July beside me, singing the grinding-corn song; Delilah, cradling her boy, Samson, at the end of the day; Little Pete, offering me cool water from the well.

I gazed at Smiling Deer and remembered Mama's pleasant ways. But as soon as the *Mekko* came through the door, those thoughts left me. His name was Chief Strong Bear and I knew why. Everything about him was big: his arms, his legs, his belly, his voice. Around his neck he wore a necklace from which swung a piece of what looked like tin, shiny and fashioned in the shape of a half-moon.

Pa and Chief Strong Bear shook hands. "Sit down." The chief motioned.

Abraham snuck back into the house and nudged me. "He talks English."

"It is said that you are a brave man," he said to Pa. "That you killed an alligator that was as big as a man," his voice bellowed.

"Yessir, 'tis true."

"And that your wife is dead and your children are without a mama."

"Also true."

"Why did you run?" Chief Strong Bear asked.

"Master was 'bout to send my youngins off."

"And you came to the swamp?"

"Lookin' for y'all. I was told you might be willin' to help us," Pa said.

The chief studied us for a spell before he stood up and spoke. "You may stay here for as long as you care to, as long as you live in peace with my people—forever, if need be. If slave hunters come, I will tell them you are my slaves and that I bought you from the Spaniards. But know that you are free to come and go as long as no trouble trails behind you. The girl will help the women with their work and learn their ways while you and the boy learn the ways of our men. The Breath Maker tells me you were sent here to take the place of three of my people who were lost to fever less than a fortnight ago."

"Who be the Breath Maker?" Abraham mumbled.

"The Lord above," Smiling Deer answered.

It was closer to morning than evening by the time we laid down to rest. "They ain't heathens like folks say," Pa said.

"Mama sure woulda fancied this place," Abraham moaned.

Pa rubbed his head. "You right, son . . . you sure is."

 FOURTEEN

Little ones follow
Into the water
Ball made of fur
Splash, splash

When we woke up, the rain was falling gently, misting the air, while everyone in the village went about their chores. Pa and Abraham went off with the men and I stayed close to Smiling Deer. "Come . . . meet my mama," she said. We scurried through the village to her mama's house while Smiling Deer lifted her face to the clouds. "The rain kisses my face."

Tiny drops covered my face as I held it to the sky.

"This is my mama, Golden Fox," she said as we entered her house.

I could see why they called her Golden Fox. Her golden skin glimmered.

"Good morning, Sally Little Song," she said as she greeted me in English.

"The words in the village fly like the wind," Smiling Deer said.

"My name be Sally Harrison," I explained.

"Well, Sally Harrison, this day you stay with me. I have many deer hides here." She pointed at a pile of skins.

"She will teach you," Smiling Deer said. Before she left, she added, "Golden Fox is wise. Listen to her words."

"Yes'm," I said.

"Today we will make the dry skins soft. Can you say *eco*?"

"Yes'm, *eco*."

"Deer, *eco*, they are the same." She reached in a bowl, picked up something with her hand, and began rubbing the deerskin. "The brain of the deer," she said, making circular motions. "Makes it soft."

"The brain?" I asked. "Like is inside my skull?"

"Yes," Golden Fox replied as she handed me a deer hide.

It still had little clumps of hair on it. As I rubbed it with the brain of the deer, some of the hair stuck to my fingers. Before long, I was done in, and I yawned.

"It is early morning and already you are weary," she observed.

"Yes'm," I replied as children ran by, playing. "I had the fever . . . a bad one. Mama said I'd likely be weak a spell." I gazed at the laughing children.

"Then go, Sally Harrison, and play with the little ones. And when the Breath Maker has made you strong again, return to my *cuko*."

I asked, "You don't think I's a lazy gal, does you? 'Cause I'm a real good worker."

"I think you are tired from the fever, as you say," she said. "Go now and catch the little ones. But if you get winded, sit and rest."

I lingered under a tree as the little ones kicked a ball made from fur along the creek bed. They chased it into the water, splashing, their giggles flying around everywhere. After a while, they scrambled up trees and rested in the branches, all the while being tended to by two Indian girls who seemed to be about my age.

The one who looked the oldest came up to me and spoke. *"Nacomeyc-ick-a?"* she asked.

"I only talks English," I told her.

Then she began counting on her fingers and I figured she wanted to know how old I was. So, I picked up a twig and made twelve marks in the dirt.

She counted them and said, *"Palen hokkolohkaken."*

It was a long word, but I reckoned it meant "twelve," so I said, "Twelve."

She smiled, pointed at her chest, and repeated, "Twelve," as if to say she was twelve too. Then she covered two marks with her hands, touched the hem of the other girl's skirt, and said, *"Palen."*

"Ten," I told her.

"Ten," both girls echoed. The younger one approached me curiously and touched my hair. My many braids had come undone and the water had shrunk my woolly hair.

Suddenly the ten-year-old ran into the brush back toward the village. The older one sat down on a huge rock and

I joined her. I wanted to ask her what her name was, but I didn't know how. So instead, we sat silently, keeping our eyes on the small gals and boys as one by one they climbed down from the trees.

Just as they began a game of tag, the other girl appeared out of the thicket, returning from the village. In her hands, she held a comb and a jar. Whatever was inside the jar smelled the same as the bear fat Smiling Deer had given me last night. She sat down behind me and rubbed the oil that had the scent of honeysuckle into my hair and combed it through. When she was finished, I parted my hair into sections and braided my hair into many small braids.

We walked along, tending the little ones, until it was time to eat the noontime meal. I followed them back to the village, where Smiling Deer and Golden Fox welcomed me to the table.

"Welcome, Sally Harrison," Golden Fox said. She set a bowl of corn soup before me.

"Thank you, ma'am," I replied, and bowed my head to pray.

Golden Fox spoke to all of the women and children in the Seminole tongue. Smiling Deer sat beside me, explaining in English what was being said. "Our harvest has left us enough food for this village and three more. We'll not be hungry come winter, and for this we must give thanks to the Breath Maker, the spirit who gives us life."

Golden Fox took her seat and everyone began to eat. I grabbed a piece of bread off a platter, but before I took a bite, I asked Smiling Deer, "What kinda bread is this?"

"Seminole bread, some call it *coontie* bread."

I took a bite. "Don't taste like pone bread, hoecakes neither," I said, glancing at Smiling Deer. I studied the faces of those at the table, all the while wishing my mama was sitting next to me. I dabbed at my eyes to keep the tears from falling.

Golden Fox motioned and said softly, "Fill your belly, Sally Harrison. The *coontie* bread and *sofkee* will make you strong."

"Yes, ma'am," I replied.

Smiling Deer told me that the two girls I'd spent the morning hours with at the creek tended the little ones and that the older one was named Turtle Lily because though she was as shy as a turtle, she was as pretty as a water lily. The ten-year-old, she said, was called Laughing Dove.

"Ain't them little ones got no work to do?" I asked between sips of soup, remembering the pails of water I'd toted since the age of four, the cotton I'd picked, the corn I'd shucked.

"Their work is to play until they tire of playing. Then, when they are men and women, they will not run from work."

After the meal I decided not to go with Turtle Lily, Laughing Dove, and the small ones who grinned a lot. Instead, I looked high and low, near and yonder, for my pa, but I couldn't find him. So I went back to Smiling Deer and asked, "You see'd my pa or my brother, Abraham?"

"They are with the men," she replied.

I tagged along beside her. "Doin' what?"

"The work of men. Some are trappers, others traders, all hunt and fish, some make canoes."

"Canoes?" I asked.

"What you call boats. Like the one that brought you here?" she answered.

She was toting a basket filled with what looked like small green apples. It seemed like there was food everywhere. "Y'all sure got a heap of vitlins."

"The Breath Maker provides."

"What's them?" I asked, pointing in the basket.

"Pond apples."

My belly was still full, but my mouth watered because I fancied apples. "Could I take one?"

"Yes, but mostly we feed them to our animals."

I grabbed a pond apple from the basket, but as soon as

I bit into it, I spit it out. "This ain't no apple!" It tasted like turpentine.

Smiling Deer laughed. "That is why we feed them to the animals."

"That all you feed 'em?"

"No, we also feed them corn that we grow."

"What else y'all grow?"

"We have many crops," she replied.

"But no cotton?" I asked, hoping she'd say no.

"No cotton. Mostly corn," she said, pointing to the ears of yellow corn that lay in rows on the ground, baking in the sun. "But it is already picked and the Green Corn ceremony is one full moon behind us."

I shook my head. "Green Corn ceremony? Corn ain't green."

" 'Tis green until harvesttime and then we celebrate, feasting on sweet ripe corn. During the ceremony some boys are given their second names, the women dance the Turtle Shell dance, marriages are made, and punishment is given those who have broken our laws."

"If'n y'all needs a corn grinder, I knows how to work the grindin' machine," I said.

"Our corn we grind by hand," Smiling Deer said.

"Could you learn me?"

"I will," she answered.

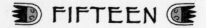 FIFTEEN

Pumpkin soup
Warm and sweet
From the bowl I sip
Sun has set
No moon tonight
The fire is always lit

P a, Abraham, and I slumbered in one of the *chickees* that night, filling the chilly evening with tales of the day.

"Abraham and me gonna havta build us our own little house," Pa said.

"Cain't we stay here?" I asked.

"Naw, gal, this'n b'longs to another, Smiling Deer's brother. He's off to the tradin' post," he replied.

Abraham wrapped a blanket around his shoulders, yawned, and said, "We's spozed to start t'morrow."

I nudged him with my elbow. "Why you so tired?"

" 'Cause today we was learned boat makin' . . . and it weren't easy," Abraham replied.

"They's made from cypress trees," Pa said.

"So y'all was choppin' down trees?" I asked, picturing Pa with an ax.

"Naw, they mostly use ones that already fallen down. They say it ain't right to chop down trees 'less you has to. So it ain't the tree choppin' but the hollowin' out that be mighty hard," Pa added as he put his head back on the straw bed. "But I can say to the Lord, I's surely blessed."

I couldn't believe my ears. "How could you say you's blessed? Mama's dead!" I cried.

"Settle down, gal . . . lemme explain. I means I's blessed with plenty work to keep my mind off your mama."

"Work sure do keep your mind off the sadness," Abraham agreed.

I felt ashamed. "I didn't do nuthin' today, 'cept mostly play."

Abraham teased me for the first time since Mama had died. "You gonna be just like January July . . . a lazy gal who cain't sing a lick."

"Only 'cause Golden Fox told me to," I protested.

"Told you what?" Pa asked.

"Play till I's strong again."

"And is you strong yet?" Abraham asked.

"Cain't say, but I knows one thing . . . I don't never wanna touch them deer brains again."

Abraham shrieked, "Deer brains!"

"Yes indeed . . . to make the hides soft."

"Then I cain't say I blames you, Sally girl. But these peoples got their ways and we each gotta learn 'em," Pa said. "Same as if they'd come to live on the plantation."

"They woulda picked cotton?" I asked.

"Sur'nuf, and caught the whip if'n they was slow 'bout it," Pa replied.

"Thissa lot better'n the plantation," said Abraham.

"But it ain't heaven," I told them.

"Naw, gal, it ain't heaven, but least we's free. . . ." Pa's voice trailed off as he covered himself with the blanket, and I knew before long he'd be asleep.

Before I closed my eyes, I thought about Mama, and it seemed like I could hear her voice plain as day, teaching me the ways of the plantation.

"When Master, the Missy, or the foremen pass by, always lower your eyes."

"Try and look busy . . . e'en if you ain't."

"Always do as you's told and be quick about it."

I missed her something terrible.

Outside, bullfrogs croaked, an owl hooted, and I slowly fell asleep.

When the sun brought a new day, the smell of food carried us to the village center, where two wild turkeys were roasting. Abraham licked his lips. "Have mercy!"

"For supper," Smiling Deer said as she tended the fire. "But there is hot *sofkee*, warm *coontie* bread, and dried deer meat."

"Thank you kindly," Pa said as he picked up the ladle and lowered it into the *sofkee*. "This all you do, cook?"

Smiling Deer took the ladle from his hand and replied, "It is my work. Sit. Sally, come . . . we will serve."

"Sally servin' me? Might be heaven after all," Abraham teased.

"Hush up, big feets," I told him. "If'n I was to give you a name, I'd call you Abraham Big Feets."

Golden Fox strutted up behind me and asked, "Has the Breath Maker made you strong yet, Sally Harrison?"

"Is you done with them deer hides?" I asked.

"I am waiting for you . . . we will finish them together."

I still felt weak from the fever and I wanted to tell her so, but instead I said, "I's stronger today than yesterday."

"But not strong enough?"

"No, ma'am, I ain't."

"Then hurry . . . fill your belly and search for Turtle Lily and Laughing Dove. Stay with them as they tend the little ones. Tomorrow, I will ask again."

"T'morrow, thank you, ma'am," I replied.

Smiling Deer spoke to Pa as she refilled his bowl with *sofkee*. "My mama, Golden Fox, is the sister of our chief, Strong Bear."

"They's both mighty strong," Pa observed.

"Strong but wise," Smiling Deer said. Then she stared into Pa's eyes and asked, "I hear you are to build a house?"

"Yes'm," he replied. "Me and my boy, we start today."

"Then you have decided to stay and live among my people."

 138

"Sur'nuf."

An Indian man sauntered by and called out to us, *"Estonko!"*

*"Estonko,"* Smiling Deer replied. "He says, 'Hello,' " she explained.

*"Estonko,"* Abraham repeated. "I could say that."

The Indian's eyes were big and slanted like a deer's, his skin smooth and reddish brown, his teeth pearly white. The bridge of his nose was high, his nostrils narrow, his shoulders broad. "He's real handsome. How you say 'handsome'?" I asked her.

*"S-im-anack-i."* I tried to say it but stumbled with the word.

Pa gestured toward the handsome Indian and asked Smiling Deer, "Is he your beau?"

Smiling Deer lowered her head, replied, "I am not yet spoken for," and walked away.

"Why you ask her that?" I said as I sat down beside him.

Pa looked ashamed and dropped his eyes. "Curious is all."

I took a sip of *sofkee* and remembered how men on the plantation never waited too long before they picked up with another woman after their missus died. Mama had said it was because men and being alone was like bitter and sweet. I wondered what was in Pa's mind, if he was as lonely for

Mama as I was. I gazed at Smiling Deer, the hem of her skirt as it brushed along. Mama would have called her comely.

After I ate, I scurried away from the village. I searched for Turtle Lily, Laughing Dove, and the little ones, but couldn't find them anywhere. So I walked along the bank of the creek by myself, until up in the distance I caught sight of a mangy red wolf standing over its kill. I halted, trying not to make a sound.

When the wolf had finished its meal, it crossed to the other side of the wide creek and disappeared into the green thicket. I stepped through the brush, stopping at the place where the wolf had been. Beautiful white feathers were strewn everywhere around a bird's bloody body. I picked up four of the feathers, and tiptoed past it. I wondered what other wild creatures were lurking about.

Suddenly, in the near distance I heard the sound of voices speaking English. I ducked into the brush and watched. It was two white men and three Indian men. The Indians talked to the white men with their hands. It seemed like they were making some sort of deal. They handed the white men what looked like a heap of alligator skins and deer hides. In return the white men presented them with a rifle.

"*Mato*," the Indians said.

"Thank you," the white men said. They loaded the hides into their boat and paddled away. I hoped they weren't slave hunters.

The Indians ran their hands over the rifle. Then one of them took it and held it above his head, like it was a prize, before they disappeared into the brush.

The sight of white men so close to this place where Pa had claimed we were free scared me. I sat frozen and quiet until I figured they were long gone. Carefully, I rose to my feet, but as I did, the wind blew one of the feathers out of my hand and I chased it as it danced through the air.

All of a sudden, a little boy tagged me as if to say I was it and scampered away like a squirrel. The others were close by, including Turtle Lily and Laughing Dove. Turtle Lily approached me cautiously. She removed a strand of her beads from her neck, slipped them over my head, and called me by my name, "Sally."

Some of the beads were made from what looked like melon seeds, others from colored glass. "They's real pretty," I said as I touched them with my fingers. "I never had nuthin' pretty. Thank you."

Laughing Dove touched her beads and said, *"Kona-wa."*

"Beads," I replied.

Laughing Dove echoed, "Beads."

I offered both of them a bird feather, and as we trailed single file back to the village, they sang songs in the Seminole tongue.

I rushed up to Smiling Deer, showing off my beads. "Turtle Lily gave me these, ain't they pretty?"

"Pretty," she replied.

I fingered one of the beads. "This'n right here look like a seed."

"Made from a melon seed."

"Back home they got watermelons, but we calls 'em August hams, and I got these here white feathers from a bird what was killed by a wolf."

"From an egret. They will bring a good price at the trading post."

"Then," I whispered, "I see'd two white men."

"Where?" she asked.

I pointed. "Yonder."

"American soldiers . . . or slave hunters?"

"Naw . . . I see'd 'Merican soldiers afore and them weren't no soldiers. First the Indians gived 'em a pile of skins, then the white men handed 'em a rifle."

"Gun traders," Smiling Deer replied. "They give the Seminoles rifles, but no powder to make them fire. You must be careful."

"Oh . . . I's careful of white folks," I told her.

"Not just white folks. Be wary of Indians from other villages too. Some are not kind and some will sell you back into slavery."

"Why come?" I asked.

"For guns and trinkets—the white man's coins."

"I'll be careful as could be," I promised.

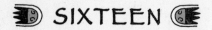 SIXTEEN

Called a *chickee*
I know why
Looks like a bird
That sure cain't fly

$S$miling Deer took me to find Pa. I asked what had happened to the two Indians who had rescued us. I hadn't seen them since the first night.

"You see'd Tall and Stout?" I asked.

"Tall and Stout?"

"Them two that found us and brought us here."

"Night Wolf and Little Panther?"

"I spoze that's what they's called, but I ain't seen 'em since we got here."

"They are away on a long hunt with the chief and most of the braves. They left the morning after you came, but when they return, they will bring with them enough to feed us through the winter: rabbits, deer, bear meat, alligator."

"Pa said y'all eat gators?"

"*Alpata.* Yes," Smiling Deer replied.

"I ate it once, but I ain't eatin' no gator never again."

"Because one killed your mama?"

"Sur'nuf . . . I gits sad and afeared every time I thinks of it. If'n she didn't fall down, it likely woulda chomped me clear in two—maybe e'en swallowed me whole."

"She saved your life by giving hers?"

I sighed. "Yes'm, I reckon."

"You long for her," she said. My eyes got watery. "Her spirit will protect you," Smiling Deer said softly.

"How could that be so? Likely she's already in heaven."

"It could be as you say, but my people believe that the spirits of those who have died before us stay on to watch over us."

I pondered this. "Maybe y'all Indians be right and us too. Maybe she could leave heaven whenever she pleases. Maybe God gave her wings same as angels."

"Maybe," Smiling Deer said.

When we came to the spot where Abraham was working, Smiling Deer turned and headed back to the village. Abraham greeted me. "What you doin' here, lazy Sally?"

"Hush your mouth, big feets. Where's Pa?"

"Totin' logs for this here house with Running Boar. He's the youngest son of the chief and if'n you ask me can he run, I'll say yes indeed, faster'n a cottontail rabbit."

"Faster'n a bobcat?" I asked.

"Yes, indeed. Where'd you git them beads? You steal 'em?"

"I ain't no thief. You knows that."

"Sally girl!" Pa said from behind me. He set down the log he was carrying. I ran to him; he held me tight, then lifted me up high. "You come to help us?" he asked, putting me down.

"Nossir, I's still playin'." I plopped down on a pile of leaves that were shaped like fans. "These for the roof, huh?"

"Yes'm," Pa said.

"Why come they builds their houses up off the ground, on legs?"

"In case the water rises."

"They looks like chicken legs," I told him. "You spoze that's why they calls 'em *chickees*?"

"Cain't say," Pa answered, pounding one piece of wood into the ground with another.

"Saw two white men," I finally told him.

Pa whipped around. "Where?"

"By the river, but they wasn't slave hunters. Smiling Deer told me they was traders."

Pa looked toward the river. "Where there's one white man, there's sure to be more. We best beware. Y'all keep your eyes and ears open, hear me?"

"Yessir," we replied.

I watched them as they toiled under the sun. Soft breezes blew through the tall blue-green grass. After a while, Abraham stopped working and sat down beside me. He offered me a piece of meat. "Bear meat, tastes good too. Want some?"

"Naw." I stood up and said, "I'll leave you be."

"Where you headin', gal?" Pa asked.

"Found a pond this mornin'."

"Fulla fish?" Abraham asked.

"Not that I could see. I's just gonna sit and talk to Mama." Pa stared at me. Abraham looked away into the distance. "She be everywhere I is, protectin' me. Least that's what Smiling Deer told me."

Tears got in Pa's eyes. "Go on then, but be careful now."

The sky was only blue, no clouds in sight. As I made my way, the wind began to blow the day cool and I shivered, wondering if a fever was trying to catch me again. I came to the pond where it was as quiet as could be, sat on a rock, and talked to my mama.

"I knows I cain't see you . . . and if'n you cain't see me, I spoze I should tell you that I's dressed like a Indian now, not like no slave gal no more.

"Thissa real pretty place and I gits to play long as I wants to, but mostly when the little ones is havin' their fun, I just lingers. You was right 'bout the fever. I been tired a good while.

"Abraham don't like to say too much 'bout you 'cause he's beaten down 'bout it, and I sees Pa cryin' most ev'ry night. I misses you terrible but hopes you fancies heaven and that it's just like Delilah always made it out to be."

The calm was broken by an egret that circled in the air,

landed nearby, and waded into the water. It had long black legs that reminded me of twigs. I studied its white feathered body and yellow bill, the way it stepped high in the water. I was sitting as still as could be to keep from scaring it off when two white-tailed deer tiptoed out of the brush toward the pond, their ears twitching this way and that. When the egret flapped its wide wings, the deer darted away and so did I.

# ⟫ SEVENTEEN ⟪

In my face
Wind blows
Up above
Clouds come
In the distance
Wolves howl

The next morning the wind was blowing hard, and just after the sun peeked into the cloudy sky, I hurried to the cooking *chickee* to eat and then to the *cuko* of Golden Fox. It was time for me to work.

"Sally Little Song," she greeted me as she sat on the floor, rubbing deer brain into the hides in circular motions.

"It's Sally Harrison, ma'am," I reminded her, even though I knew most of them in the village referred to me as Sally Little Song in their Seminole tongue. I figured they most likely thought I didn't understand, but I did.

She corrected herself. "Sally Harrison, I see you are stronger and have tired of playing."

"Naw . . . but Turtle Lily and Laughing Dove, they cain't talk no real English."

"And you like to talk?"

"Yes'm, always did," I replied, picking up a deerskin, humming a tune. "Like this?" I asked as I pressed the brain of the deer into the hide, hard and hurriedly.

Golden Fox took my hand and guided it. "A soft, gentle motion."

A question I'd been waiting to ask came to my tongue. "How come you and Smiling Deer talks proper, like white folks? Her pa was a colored runaway, weren't he?"

"He was, but my mama was a white woman."

"How'd she get here?"

"Her papa was a trapper, well known to my people. One day when he came, he had his daughter with him. She was about your age, and he told our chief that her mother had been killed by smallpox. He left her here, saying he would be back, but didn't return for many moons. Then word came that he had been killed by a bear and so she stayed, learned our ways, and became the wife of my papa."

"That's how come you's yella," I told her.

"Golden," she replied.

I worked alongside her, stopping only once to relieve myself, neither of us going to the noontime meal. Just before sunset I finished one entire skin. I held it up proudly for her to see, and said, "I's dun . . . what's the next thing you gotta learn me?"

"One skin, you think is enough?"

"Sure do, you teached and I learned. I's quick-witted is what Mama used to say."

"Last night I asked the Breath Maker to give me wisdom about Sally Harrison who is new to our ways," Golden Fox said.

"And what'd he say?"

"The Breath Maker said here is a girl who has only

known work, a girl who longs for her mama, who though she is as tall as many a woman, in her heart remains a little one."

"He said all that?"

"Yes . . . and so I have decided."

Suddenly I got fearful and interrupted, "Y'all ain't gonna make us leave 'cause I was too tired to work, is you? 'Cause thissa heap better'n the plantation."

"Don't be afraid, Sally. I have decided that one day you will work and the next you will play until the Breath Maker reveals to me that your heart is no longer the heart of a little one."

"So t'morrow I gets to play or I could stay with Pa and Abraham while they builds our house?"

"The day is yours, spend it as you please."

"Much obliged," I said as I stood to leave.

"And Sally Harrison . . . when your face greets me at sunrise on the day that follows the next, I hope it comes with a smile."

"Maybe so," I replied, and ran to search for Pa and Abraham. I found them at the creek, where they stood waist-deep in water. "Hey!" I yelled.

"Don't come no closer, Sally, 'cause we's in the altogether!" Pa called out.

Abraham added, "Naked as two newborn pigs."

"Close your eyes, gal," Pa said, "whilst we comes out the water and gets dressed."

"Yessir," I replied, and waited. But the sounds of horses' hooves made me turn around. At first I could hardly see because it was dusk. Then, as they got closer, I saw them: three white men on horses, headed our way.

When I finally saw their faces, I shuddered. Two of the men I'd seen before. Once outside the shed when January July and I were grinding corn. The second time with the hounds when Mama, Pa, Abraham, and I had hidden in the tree.

Slave hunters.

Pa and Abraham had dressed and were walking toward me, but I ran to them and grabbed their hands, pulling them into the brush. "Shhh," I whispered, and pointed. "Slave hunters."

We hid, hoping they would ride past us. But their horses led them to water. I shook like a leaf in the wind as one slid off his saddle. "We'll let the horses rest a spell b'fore we head back to camp. Nuthin' out here but swamp and critters anyway," the one with red hair said.

"There's Indians . . . nearby, I know it," the second declared as he climbed down off his horse. "They're quieter'n ghosts." He yanked the reins of his horse and led it to the

158

creek's edge to drink. "Then outta nowhere, an arrow flies straight at your heart."

"I ain't a braggart," the third one bellowed, waving the night swamp bugs away with his hat, "but for as long as I've been slave huntin' and scoutin' about, no Indian's arrow has ever pierced my skin."

"Seth," the first man called him by name, "how long you been huntin'?"

"A lot longer'n you, Irish Red, but I never been this deep into the swamp."

"Why ya always call me Irish Red? My given name's Jack and you know it."

" 'Cause your pa was Irish and that crop of hair growing atop your head looks mighty red to me," the one I'd never seen before replied.

Their laughter filled the air as one of the horses finished drinking and wandered away from the water. It stood right in front of us, sniffing us out like it was part hound. When the horse stepped on Abraham's bare foot, Abraham let out a howl that made the slave hunters grab their rifles and come running.

We crouched down, but as they poked into the bushes with their bayonets, one of them pierced my shoulder. I squealed in pain as the blood trickled down my arm.

"Show yourselves. And if you're armed, put your weapons down!" the one named Seth yelled.

"We ain't armed," Pa said as he took Abraham and me by the hands and led us out of the brush.

Seth laughed like someone had told him a joke as we stood before them. "Well, ain't this a sight, niggers dressed up like Indians."

"Y'all the ones we've been huntin'—off the Harrison plantation?" the eldest asked.

"Nossir, we was bought from the Spaniards by the chief of this village and we b'longs to him."

Jack nudged Seth. "Indians with slaves, you believe that?"

"I've heard talk of it," the one I'd never seen before replied. "Colored and Indian livin' side by side in harmony. More like brothers than master and slave. Most likely Seminoles, from what I've been told."

"Yessir, they be Seminoles," Pa answered. Blood was dripping from my fingers. "If'n you'd be so kind, I'd like to get my little gal back to the village so's we can look after her arm," Pa begged.

"By the way, what's the name of this chief?" Seth asked.

Abraham answered, "Chief Strong Bear."

"That so?" the eldest asked before he added, "Y'all don't mind if we follow you, do you?" We must have looked frightened, because he asked, "What's the matter? If you're speakin' the truth, we mean you no harm."

"No harm," Jack repeated.

"We'll trail behind you back to the village so we can have us a talk with Chief Strong Bear."

"That won't hardly be possible!" Abraham blurted.

They pointed their rifles at us. " 'Cause the truth is that you're the runaways we've been huntin' and Chief Strong Bear is just someone you dreamed up to keep us from collectin' our bounty?"

"Naw, 'cause him and most the other braves dun gone off on a long hunt," Abraham replied.

Something in Seth's eyes spelled trouble. "So it's mainly women and children in the village tonight?"

Abraham had his mouth open to answer when Pa spoke up. "The village still got plenty braves."

"That a fact?" Seth asked.

"Yessir," Pa replied, knowing that there were only three at best.

They climbed up on their horses and pointed their bayonets at our backs.

My arm was still bleeding and hurt something awful. I wanted to cry out as we headed toward the light from the fire that burned day and night in Chief Strong Bear's village.

"Sally girl, fall to the ground," Pa whispered.

"Huh?" I said.

"Fall to the ground . . . pretendin' you dun passed out."

"Like I got the fever?"

"Fever, sur'nuf, to bide some time."

I sank to the grass.

The slave hunters stopped their horses and aimed their bayonets. "What's wrong with the gal?" the one named Seth asked.

Pa lied, "Musta passed out . . . she dun lost a heap of blood."

"Here, tie this around her arm, should stop the bleeding," Jack said, handing Pa a kerchief.

Pa tightened the kerchief around my arm.

"Can you carry her?" the one called Jack asked.

"Yessir, I sur'nuf could." Pa smiled and nodded, acting like he was back on the Harrison plantation, standing in front of the overseer.

Pa picked me up.

"I see a fire," Seth declared. "That the village?"

"Yessir," Pa replied.

Pa carried me, stumbling along, Abraham beside us, the men so close, I could feel the warmth of their horses' breath. All I could think was that we had found us a hundred troubles by running away.

"Look what we have here," Seth said when he saw the first *chickee*, "a little straw house."

"Them's leaves, not straw," Abraham sassed.

Jack poked Abraham in the back with his bayonet, not enough to draw blood but just enough to make him shout. Pa whispered, "Hush, boy, afore they slips a rope round your neck."

Right then I remembered Abraham's dream, when he saw himself hanging from a tree. I lifted my head from Pa's shoulder and squinted at the men. They each had one, hanging ropes.

My cut had stopped bleeding but there was a trail of dried red blood from my shoulder to my hand. We made our way to the center of the village, where the Indians were all gathered around the fire. Some of the little ones were asleep in their mamas' arms.

Pa put me down right outside the *chickee*, and the Indians, old and young, grinned at us until they glimpsed the horses.

The men who rode them.

The guns aimed our way.

The dread on our faces.

Then, faster than the snap of a finger, Running Boar and the two other braves leaped up and ran into the darkness. Seth turned his horse and galloped after them.

 163

The eldest white man spoke. "We come in peace and to meet your chief, Strong Bear."

The Indians stared at him blankly, including Golden Fox and Smiling Deer, as if they didn't understand English.

"English . . . anyone other'n these coloreds here speak English?" he asked.

The Indians glanced around at each other.

Jack jabbed at Pa with his bayonet. "You speak Indian?"

"Nossir, ain't been here long enough to be teached," Pa replied.

He stared at Abraham. "What about you?"

Abraham shook his head no.

"And you?"

"Me, sir?" I asked.

"Yes, you."

I trembled. "Nossir, I onliest knows some words. *Alpata,* that be same as 'gator,' plus I knows the words for deer and beads, and that house you called straw, they calls it a *cuko* or a *chickee.*"

Golden Fox approached them with a basket of *coontie* bread, offered it to the slave hunters, and motioned for them to sit on the floor, at the table. "Inviting us to supper," Redheaded Jack said. "Ain't that sweet?"

All of a sudden Seth's horse trotted back, panting and shaking its head, but Seth was missing from its saddle. Jack and the other man pointed their rifles at the Indians. "Seth!" they yelled.

I thought I heard footsteps behind me and I glanced around, expecting to see Seth, but I didn't see anyone. Then I remembered what the slave hunters had said about Indians being quieter than ghosts.

An arrow flew, headed straight at Jack, but missed. Then another. Jack aimed at the Indians inside the *chickee*, but Pa jumped him. The rifle fired as it fell to the ground, sending its shot into the air.

The older man aimed his rifle at Abraham and the rest of us who had huddled together. "Next one who moves is dead," he warned.

Jack and Pa wrestled on the ground. Jack pulled out a knife and Pa struggled to pry it out of his hand. Suddenly, Jack twisted in pain. Somehow the knife had found its way into his chest. Jack gasped for breath, then lay still.

"Stand up, nigger," the other slave hunter commanded.

"I weren't tryin' to kill him," Pa panted, trying to catch his breath.

"Weren't tryin', but you did."

"You gonna shoot me, sir?" Pa asked.

"Got to," he answered. "Turn around, take it in the back."

Abraham leaped at the man, but the slave hunter

tripped him. When Abraham fell, he turned his gun on him. "You or the boy," he said to Pa.

"Me," Pa replied, "but not in the back. You gonna shoot me, I wanna see it comin'."

The white man put his finger on the trigger.

And that was when the arrows hit him.

Three at once.

He slumped to the ground and moaned. Pa grabbed the rifle and stood over him. The man's head fell to one side.

His eyes were wide-open.

Dead.

Running Boar and the two other braves crept up behind Pa, bows in hand. "There were only three?" Running Boar asked.

"Only three," Pa replied. "Two right here . . . other one's horse came back without him."

"He breathes no more," Running Boar replied.

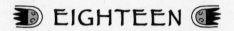 EIGHTEEN

Pa got courage
He so brave
Him by my side
I feel safe

Smiling Deer and Golden Fox washed the blood off my arm and rubbed salve on it, but it still pained me. Pa left me with Abraham while he went off with the braves, probably to bury the men's bodies. I crawled into a corner of the *chickee* and wrapped my blanket around me. I was sure more slave hunters were on their way and I wanted to have both eyes open. Without Pa around, I was mighty scared.

Abraham was flat on his back, but I didn't think he was sleeping. "What else gonna happen?" I asked.

"Cain't say, Sally. Nuthin' bad, I hope."

"Pa been gone a long spell," I told him.

"Too long," he replied.

"Maybe he's lost," I said.

"Not likely."

I went to the door and looked around. The moon was big, round, bright. "I'ma go find him," I told Abraham. "You comin'?"

Abraham jumped up. "Sur'nuf."

We tiptoed through the village until we found ourselves at the *cukŏ* where the fire blazed day and night. The chief and many other men, including Pa, were gathered there.

Abraham and I crouched down out of sight, peered inside, and listened.

"They's back from huntin'," I whispered.

Abraham replied, "Picked a fine time."

For the first time, I saw other colored men. Some looked older than my pa, some looked younger. All were dressed like braves. The men were talking quietly among themselves until the chief stood up. Then there was silence.

"Titus Harrison," he said, and motioned for him to stand. "You are a very brave man."

Pa nodded his head and said, "Thank you kindly."

"Your courage has led me to make you and your boy and girl child members of my clan. And to bestow upon you the name Great Horse . . . Titus Great Horse."

"Abraham Great Horse . . . got a nice ring," Abraham said softly.

Some of the men echoed, "Titus Great Horse."

Chief Strong Bear reached to embrace Pa. "Welcome, brother . . . Titus Great Horse."

Pa hesitated. "Chief Strong Bear, I's happy to be welcomed to your clan and to be gived a Indian name. From what I been told t'night, thissa honor only gived to a few and the name Great Horse sounds mighty fine, but if'n I could pick a name for m'self and my youngins, I would be obliged to take the name Little Song out of respect to my Dessa."

The chief and Pa stared at each other for what felt like a long time. Finally Chief Strong Bear spoke. "Titus Little Song . . . welcome, brother."

The chief embraced Pa and while some of the men cheered, others sat in silence. It seemed like the meeting was about over and I grabbed Abraham's hand and pulled him to his feet. "C'mon, 'fore they sees us."

Abraham smiled as we took the footpath back to the *chickee.* "Abraham Little Song." He stopped walking and did a jig. "I's a Indian now, e'en got me a Indian name, Abraham Little Song."

"Sally Little Song," I whispered. Then I smiled and said it louder. "Sally Little Song."

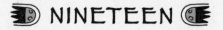 NINETEEN

Many feathers
Bearskin coat
Iron legs
He struts

At sunrise, I saw the dead men's horses grazing in the tall grass, the bloodstains in the *chickee,* worried looks on some of the Indians' faces. I wondered if any of them wished we'd never come to their village. I hoped not. I fingered my capelike blouse. I liked this place and fancied these people. Though I longed for my mama, though I missed Delilah, Old Moses, January July, and colored food, though I still felt like a stranger here, I wanted to stay.

I glanced around and saw some of the same colored men I had seen last night.

"Hey, little gal," one with hardly any teeth in his mouth said when I sat down to eat. He reminded me of Old Moses. "Where you come from?"

"Georgia, way north of Waycross."

"You Titus's gal?"

"Yessir, I's Sally," I replied, figuring he'd talked to Pa last night.

"Your pa's plenty brave."

"Sure is."

"I's called Caleb."

"Caleb what?"

"Just Caleb."

"Ain't you got no Indian name?"

"No, ma'am, them's names you gotta earn . . . a honor."

"My pa earned his, Titus Little Song," I said proudly.

"So now you's Sally Little Song, a colored Indian."

"I's still colored, sir, not no Indian."

"Got on Indian clothes?" Caleb asked.

"Yessir."

"Eatin' Indian food?"

"Yessir."

"Livin' in a Indian village?"

"Reckon so."

"Seems like you be a colored Indian to me, like it or not."

I finished eating and excused myself as politely as I could. "Bye, sir." I hurried away, thinking that if I had to give him a name, it would be Caleb Many Questions.

The village was full of people. As I looked around for Pa, I saw Chief Strong Bear. He strutted toward me on legs that were like iron, wearing many feathers and a necklace that looked like three shiny crescent moons. "Daughter of Titus?" he asked.

"Yessir," I replied.

He patted the top of my head. "My sister Golden Fox smiles when she speaks of you, Sally Little Song."

"Sally—" I almost spit out the name Harrison, but

caught myself and said, "Thank you, sir," before he went on his way.

I found Pa and Abraham building our *chickee*. Smiling Deer was there too and I wondered why she wasn't off gathering pond apples or boiling the *coontie*, preparing it for bread.

She greeted me, "Good morning, Sally."

"Mornin'," I replied.

"Look what she dun brought us," Abraham said, pointing to a basket of grub.

"In case they get hungry," Smiling Deer explained as Pa worked.

"Ain't that nice'a her?" Pa said from the roof.

"Sur'nuf is," I said, watching the way she looked at my pa, like she was sweet on him. When she left, saying she had work to do, I asked Abraham, "You think she brought that 'cause of what Pa did last night, or you think she's sweet on him?"

"Some of both. Her eyes got that twinkle when she gazes at him. Plus he's Indian now, same as her."

I stared at Pa, his bare brown chest glistened with sweat. "I's goin' now, Pa."

"Where?"

"To the pond. To talk to Mama."

"Be careful, now, Sally."

A ring-necked duck was in the pond when I got there, and as I sat on a rock, I heard the tap, tap, tap of a woodpecker. Dragonflies landed on the water and then fluttered away, and two hawks soared above, seeming like they were floating on air.

"Mama, if'n you's here, I hopes you could hear me. Last night we got Indian names, but I still feels colored, like the plantation ain't too far away.

"When I went to eat this mornin', some of the Indians looked away, and I been wonderin' if the chief gonna change his mind and tell us to leave. I didn't say nuthin' to Pa 'bout it, though, cuz he would say I's bein' afeared.

"I was hopin' to learn my letters, so's I could learn to read and write, but cain't no one round here do that. I ain't see'd no books no way. Mostly they draws pictures in the dirt to explain things, so I's learnin' that.

"Thank you for watchin' over me, but I got a favor to ask. I been thinkin' 'bout January July bein' without no mama or pa. So if'n it's possible for you to watch over more'n just me, could you keep a eye on her too? But if'n you cain't, could you ask the Lord to please send a angel just for her? I'd be beholdin' to you."

A mockingbird landed on the branch of a nearby tree,

sang a little tune, and flew away. I gathered up the silence, gazed into the sky, and said, "Bye, Mama."

I followed the trail that led to the creek, where I found Turtle Lily and Laughing Dove tending the little ones, who were tossing rocks into the water, squealing and giggling every time one went plink.

"*Estonko*, Sally!" They said, waving me toward them.

I called back, "*Estonko!*" Laughing Dove and Turtle Lily both greeted me by slipping strands of beads over my head. Now I had three. I tried hard to remember the Seminole word for "thank you," and finally it slipped into my mind. "*Mato*," I told them.

They placed their hands over their mouths, but I could still see their smiles.

We spent the morning making sure the little ones didn't find too much trouble and most of the afternoon curled up with them, singing songs, cradling some of them in our arms as they napped.

When suppertime came, I left to find my pa.

The *chickee* was full of people. While we ate supper, Caleb grinned at me from across the way. Then Chief Strong Bear stood. His voice bellowed. Smiling Deer was sitting across from Pa, Abraham, and me. She explained in

English, "He says, 'I give thanks to the Breath Maker for his protection and for sending a very brave man, Titus Little Song, to our village.'"

One of the old Indian men rose from his seat and spoke. Smiling Deer frowned. "He asks, 'What if more white men come looking for runaway slaves? Our women and children are not safe.'"

A few of the other Indians nodded their heads in agreement. I glanced at Pa and Abraham. Chief Strong Bear looked at the faces of his people for a long spell and then at us. Finally, he spoke.

When he finished, Smiling Deer said, "He says . . . 'Old man, do not put fear in our people. We are Seminoles. We will never surrender to the white man or take his ways. It is why we left the Muskogee tribe and came to the big swamp. I was foolish to leave our village with so few braves. From this time on, at least ten braves will remain in the village, even during the hunting season. White men have come before and they may come again. Some will come to bring us harm . . . some will come in peace, as the father of my mother did.'"

Chief Strong Bear came over to where we were sitting and gestured for Pa to stand up. He placed his hand on Pa's shoulder and kept talking. The only words I understood were "Titus Little Song."

"The chief says that 'Titus Little Song and his boy and girl are not slaves. They are members of our clan. I have spoken,'" Smiling Deer whispered to Abraham and me.

I glanced around and saw many smiling faces.

Later that night, Smiling Deer stood near the door of the *chickee* and watched us as Pa, Abraham, and I went to our *cuko*. "She got pleasant ways," I told Pa.

"Sure do," Pa replied.

"Like Mama," I told him.

"Yes'm," was all Pa said.

I went outside, sat on the step that reminded me of the plantation cabin's narrow porch, and gazed into the sky. Clouds surrounded the moon until they swallowed it, but there it was, as bright as ever, Joshua's star.

I pondered what the chief had said, that we were not slaves. I wondered if he was right, if his words could make it so. I feared that any day or night slave hunters could show up and drag us back to the plantation.

I knew that every time I glimpsed a white man atop a horse, I would run into the brush and hide. I knew that anytime an Indian who was not from our clan approached on foot, I would wonder if he had come to sell us back into slavery. I supposed that Pa, Abraham, and I would always be watchful.

Even though we no longer carried the name Harrison

and had been given our Indian name, we still weren't free. I knew that as long as there was slavery in this place called 'Merica, Pa, Abraham, and I would never really be at ease. And neither would the Indians.

I glanced up once more at Joshua's star and said a prayer for my mama before I went back inside.

My skin is as brown as mud, my eyes as dark as the bottom of a well at night, my hair black and softer than the wool of any lamb. I am twelve years old, neither slave nor free.

My name is Sally Little Song.

# Afterword

During the 1700s refugees from the Muskogee (Creek) Nation and other Native American tribes settled in northern Florida and what is now called the Okefenokee Swamp, also known as "The Land of the Trembling Earth."

These runaways renamed themselves Seminoles, which comes from the Spanish word for "wild." The word *Seminole* has also been translated to mean "lovers of freedom."

Some Seminole chiefs bought or were given black slaves by the Spanish. For the most part, however, the slaves had considerable freedom. These slaves taught the Native Americans farming methods they had brought with them from Africa. Most notably, they taught them rice farming. Others functioned as interpreters or scouts.

Soon, slaves attempting to escape from plantations in Georgia and Alabama found their way to these Seminole camps. Many Seminole chiefs granted the escapees independence within the village but required them to pay taxes and to give the chief a portion of their crops. It was a small price to pay for freedom and the added protection the Seminoles offered them from plantation owners and bounty hunters.

Some of these "Freedmen" or "Black Indians" were given tribal membership and married into Seminole clans. Others created their own black settlements, two of them being named "Hide Me" and "Lament for Me."

*My Name Is Sally Little Song* is a fictional account of one African American family who took this route to freedom.